A Promise Broken
A Promise Kept

By Christine Egbert

Betrothed
Messianic Imprint of Little Roni Publishers, LLC
ALABAMA | TENNESSEE
www.littleronipublishers.com

ISBN: 979-8-9890806-2-5
Also available in eBook
V122052023SC

For editorial requests or to purchase multiple copies at wholesale, contact The Editor at SubmissionsLRP@gmail.com.

PUBLISHED IN THE UNITED STATES OF AMERICA

Other Works by Christine Egbert

Miracle Across the Sound
Contending for the Faith
What God is Doing

Author's Note

Although my novel is fiction, many of my characters—those associated with the Alyiah Beit and the *Exodus 1947*—are based on real-life heroes. I adapted many of their actual exploits from accounts recorded in the book *Exodus 1947* by David C. Holly, published by the Naval Institute Press.

I was so moved by what these young American Jews with little to no nautical experience committed to, in order to help displaced holocaust-survivors enter their God-given Land, I had to put some of their adversities and adventures into my sequel, *A Promise Broken & A Promise Kept.**

My character the Reverend John Bark was based on a Methodist minister named John Stanley Grauel, who loved the Lord and His Chosen people.

* Publisher's addendum: the title was altered by the publisher to *A Promise Broken A Promise Kept.* Also, we invite you to learn more on this subject at Exodus1947.com.

1917 Balfour Declaration

By the 1800s, the British Empire had grown so vast around the world it became known as "the Empire on which the sun never sets." In November of 1917, the British Foreign Affairs Secretary of State, Arthur Balfour, wrote a letter to Lord Rothschild in which he expressed his support for the establishment of a national homeland in Palestine for the Jewish people. One month later, General Sir Edmund Allenby's British and Allied forces defeated the Ottoman Empire, wresting control over the ancient city of Jerusalem. By October of the following year, the British Army controlled all of Palestine. That victory became a double-edged sword when Britain failed not only to keep its promise to the Jewish people, but it severely limited Jewish immigration quotas while increasing them for Arabs.

Yahweh promised to bless those who bless His people Israel and to curse those who curse them. It is this author's contention that God brought judgment on Great Britain for its disgraceful treatment of the Jewish people prior to, during, and after WWII, beginning in 1950 when India gained its independence. One decade later, the sun fully set on the British Empire when its Asian and African colonies did likewise.

Jeremiah 30:3

"For behold, the days are coming when I will return My people Israel and Judah from exile," declares Adonai. "I will bring them back to the land that I gave to their fathers, and they will possess it."

Prologue

John Bark, the only blonde-haired, blue-eyed member of the Hagenah's *Aliyah Beit*, known formerly as Pastor John Stanley Bark to his Methodist congregation back in Main, glanced at his watch. It was getting late. "We better get started," he said to those gathered in the tiny back room. "We've managed to smuggle only 252 refugees into Palestine in the past six months, but that's about to change because tomorrow I'm packing to head back to the States, to a snow-covered shipyard in Baltimore. There, I will be joining a novice crew of young American Jews, mostly from Brooklyn and the Bronx, along with a guy from Cincinnati and one from San Francisco."

"The Brits are gonna wet their knickers when they go up against our boys from the Bronx," Steven Greenbaum yelled from the back of the room.

"That's exactly what we're hoping," John replied, returning the proud New Yorker's smile. "The crew and I will be boarding the Hagenah's latest acquisition, an old passenger ship that ferried pleasure-cruisers from Baltimore to Norfolk in her glory days. After we've refitted the old tub, we'll christen her the *Exodus 1947* to comport with her mission."

"How many will she hold?" Bucky Rabinowitz asked.

"Up to five thousand," John said. "As an American I'm proud to report that the Jewish community in the States, who already raised a small fortune to aid Jews who are being warehoused in some of the very same camps they got liberated from, have now raised another $40,000."

"They're not just being warehoused, John," Greenbaum said. "They're crammed in with former card-carrying Nazis and quislings."

"That's why we're all here, Steven. But if everyone will settle down," John said, "I'll give you the good news. In response to David Ben Gurion's latest plea for funding, as I was saying, American Jews raised another $40,000 with which we have purchased the old *S.S. President Warfield.* And please, I hope none of you miss the irony of it being *that* particular old tub."

"What's so special about her?" Steven asked.

"She was named for S. Davies Warfield, the President of the old Baltimore Bay Line, who just happens to be uncle to that infamous divorcee Wallace Warfield Simpson who is now married England's abdicated and antisemitic King, Edward XIII. But be it the LORD's will," John continued, "we will outfit the old ship to take on thousands of displaced Jews, thereby thwarting Britain's miserly immigration quotas."

Cheering erupted throughout the room. When it finally died down, John closed their meeting then snatched his hat off the rack by the door. Then Bucky Rabinowitz stepped in front of him.

"Where are you off to? I thought we were grabbing a bite to eat."

"Eat something for me," John told him. "I'm beat. I'm hitting the sack."

Grateful that his room was only one floor up, he prayed climbing the stairs so he could drift off to sleep with a clear conscience as soon as his head hit the pillow … at least that was his plan. But as he lay on his bed his thoughts took him back to the year before. He'd just attended his first Zionist conference when the Lord opened the door to his destiny.

One

As the Jerusalem sun peeked over the horizon outside of Jacob Metzger's window another dream about Fleming Lund smuggling Jews into the land ended suddenly. Once again, Flem's wife, Liesel, and his son, Caleb, were living nearby but their exact location was never clear.

Jacob sat up and rubbed his eyes. Why was he having these dreams? And more importantly, what did they mean? Since Katlev arrived at the camp in Theresienstadt, Jacob had hardly dreamt at all, and when he did, they faded quickly. But not these! They were different. They were vivid, and they haunted him throughout the day. He must ask the Giver of dreams for discernment.

ജ്ര

Early one morning in late December of 1946, Flem arrived at the cemetery with a spring in his step because the temperature in Copenhagen had risen unseasonably, making it feel as if winter had ended instead of just begun. When he noticed all the moss creeping up the base of Katlev's monument, he dropped Liesel's flowers chiding himself. He should've come sooner…and more often.

Determined not to let this happen again, he fell on his knees.

Then a still, small voice reminded him that Katlev was only sleeping and not even in this grave. His ashes were still in Czechoslovakia.

But one day, when that last blast of a shofar sounded, Katlev would awaken in a glorified body. Like every Bible believing disciple, Flem's hope was in the Resurrection. Yeshua taught that when a grain of wheat falls to the ground and dies, it remains alone. But through that death, it produces fruit, and Katlev's sacrifice had most certainly proved it on the Sabbath Jacob Mitzger showed up on Flem's doorstep. It changed his father's life.

Flem picked up the urn and replaced the dead foliage with Liesel's daisies, then checked his watch. It was time to go, time to pound out some more obituaries. Then he would ask his boss, Geørg, for permission to write another op-ed for the *Gazette*'s editorial page.

ჱჲ

"What's wrong?" Liesel asked as Flem helped her clear away the dishes.

"Oh, nothing."

"You've hardly spoken a word tonight."

"That's not true," he said, wishing she'd drop the subject.

"If it wasn't for our son's incessant chatter we might've eaten in silence, and that's just not like you. So, stop trying to spare me and tell me what's eating you."

He stroked her cheek. "You know me too well, my beauty. You always have."

"That's better," she said with a smile. "But I still want to know why you're so pensive."

"I'm just tired," he said, hoping to not have to explain the embarrassing exchange he'd had earlier with his boss. But his wife's luminous blue eyes let him know she wasn't buying it. Flem smiled. "Okay, okay! I'll talk…I am tired, tired of doing obituaries. I want to write!"

Liesel's expression softened to the one Flem loved best. "I know you do, darling. And you will. Give it time. Why, that article you wrote a few months ago was nothing short of inspiring."

"That's just it…it was months ago. This afternoon I made the mistake of asking Geørg if I could try my hand at another one, and do you know what he told me?"

"What?"

"He reminded me in no uncertain terms that I'm a stringer and he's the editor."

"He actually said that?"

"Every word."

"But that article received tons of positive mail."

"I know," Flem said, watching the wheels turn in his lovely wife's brain. "What are you thinking?"

"Do you suppose Geørg might feel threatened by you…by the response to your article, I mean?"

"Do you think that's it?" he asked, pondering the possibility.

"Well, don't let it eat you up, Flem. The Lord is still in control.

"Thanks. I needed that little reminder." Flem lifted her chin and kissed her lips.

"If you're going up now, would you peek in on Caleb? He's been falling asleep on the floor next to his train lately."

"I will, my love. And if I'm not in bed when you come up, check my prayer room. You'll likely find me crashed out in my chair."

ꕤ

At the breakfast table the next morning, though thoroughly disgusted by the latest actions taken by the British Army in Palestine, Flem's chest filled with pride for his countrymen. He folded the morning paper and placed it on the table next to his coffee.

Liesel came over and stared at his plate. "Is something wrong?"

"Wrong? Yes! And right, too. Every Dane who joined His Majesty's 6th Airborne Division during the war has now petitioned to be excused from duty. They refuse to fight Jews in Palestine."

"You hardly ate a bite. Didn't you like it?"

"Your omelets are always exemplary. I just don't have an appetite."

"Then stop reading the newspaper at breakfast!" She scraped his leftovers into the garbage.

"I can't read it before bed. I'll never sleep."

Liesel turned and stared at him, frowning. "The war ended last year, Flem. When are you going to put it behind you?"

"The way things are looking, not anytime soon. How can I? I'm a Jew."

"You're a Christian by faith," she retorted emphatically as she refilled her coffee.

"By birth I'm a Jew and I'll always be a Jew…one who knows his Jewish Messiah."

Liesel frowned. "You know what I mean."

"Then why can't you understand how I feel?"

"I do, Flem. I just can't deal with all the strife. I'm tired of it. I want it over. I want life to go back to the way it was before the war."

"So do a quarter of a million Jews, who'll never get their life back the way it was before the war. The only thing that's changed for them is the location of the battlefield."

"Then let them immigrate someplace else so they can get on with their lives."

Flem struggled to choose his words wisely and deliver them in an even tone. "It's our homeland, min smukke."

"We're Danes. Denmark is our homeland."

"Your problem is you don't study prophecy, Liesel."

"Well, you don't have to get angry about it!" she said, looking close to tears. "I've tried. It's confusing, and it's not a salvation issue."

"Ending our exile is Israel's salvation as a nation. You'd know that if you ever bothered to open your Old Testament."

"I've tried! I just don't understand most of it."

"Can you understand justice?" he asked. "Or is that too hard for you, too?"

"Don't be insulting!"

Hating himself for his outburst, Flem took her hands. "I'm sorry, min smukke. I don't mean to take it out on you. Please forgive me."

"Don't I always?"

"You do, and I love you for it."

"That's better," she said, still sounding a bit peeved. "Now, if you can explain why you're so frustrated without being a bear, I'll listen."

Flem took a deep breath. "The British promised us a homeland, but now they're acting like Hitler's Brown Shirts for the Arabs. These are my people, Liesel, the very same people you once promised would be yours. We want a homeland, a place we can live without being exterminated. And not just any place. We want the land Elohim granted our patriarchs in an irrevocable covenant."

Tears filled his wife's eyes.

"I'm sorry, min smukke," he said, pulling her into his arms. "I'm not mad at you. I'm just angry at the injustice of it all."

"I'm sorry, too…and I meant what I said. Your people are my people. I'm just weary. I want life back the way it was before the war."

Flem pulled out his handkerchief and dried her tears. "You want it back to the way we thought it was."

"What do you mean 'thought it was?'"

"This world's been in turmoil ever since Adam and Eve got exiled from the Gan Eeden," he said using its Hebrew name. "But we were too young to realize it before the war," Flem told her as Caleb dashed into the kitchen.

He shoved them apart. "I've been calling you, but you won't answer! Uncle Aldur is at the door, and I can't reach the chain."

Two

Flem smiled down at the boy. "I'm sorry. We didn't hear you, Caleb. You and I can go and let him in."

"It's okay. I'll do it," Liesel said.

As she left the kitchen, Caleb placed his fists on his hips. "You always talk to my mother too much!"

Flem picked the child up, struggling not to laugh. "And why do you suppose that is?"

"Because you love her," he said with a pouty face.

"Ah, so you do remember."

"Yes, but you don't talk to me with so many words. Don't you love me?"

"Of course, I do," Flem assured him, amazed at the way his son's mind worked. He was about to dig deeper when Liesel returned with Aldur.

"Can I pour you a cup of coffee?" Liesel offered. "Or tea?"

Aldur shook his head. His expression looked bleak. "I just need to speak to Flem."

"Well, here he is," Liesel said.

"In private, if you don't mind."

Liesel looked surprised. "Better come with me, Caleb. We know when we're not wanted. Don't we, little man?"

Flem pulled out a chair next to his. "Have a seat, old buddy. What's going on? You look upset."

"You can't breathe a word of what I'm about to tell you, especially not to Liesel. You know how she is about the war."

Intrigued, Flem sat down.

"Last night I was working late and came across a document wedged behind a false partition at the back of a file cabinet containing immigration papers. Only what I found had nothing to do with immigration. It listed the names of every Jew seeking asylum here in Denmark between 1935 and '45."

"So, what's the problem?" Flem asked.

"Every single one of them was deported to Berlin."

"How can that be?" Flem asked. "Our people risked their lives to save Jews. You know that…you were one of them."

"We ordinary Danes risked our lives. Not our elites. Twenty-eight thousand of them were card-carrying Nazis."

"Twenty-eight thousand? Are you sure? I can't believe it."

"You don't want to believe it, and neither did I. But I saw it with my own eyes. From 1935 until last year when the war ended, every Jew reaching our shores seeking asylum was turned over to the Nazis. Right now, Helmer Rosting is relocating Nazi war criminals to South America."

"The Director of our Red Cross?"

"Before we were even occupied, several of our firms were using Jewish slave labor to build roads and fortifications for Hitler."

Flem held up his hand. "Stop! I need time to process all of this."

Aldur checked his watch. "I've got to get back to the office anyway. I've got a mountain of paperwork on my desk, and I have to leave early today to take Marlene to the doctor."

"Is she okay?" Flem asked.

For the first time since his arrival, Aldur's smile looked genuine. "She's been having morning sickness."

"Marlene is pregnant?"

"That's what we hope her doctor will confirm," Aldur said as he rose.

Flem got up too. "May I tell Liesel?"

"Absolutely! Just don't mention the rest." Aldur squeezed Flem's shoulder. "I just had to let you know right away in case you were planning to write another editorial heralding our moral superiority."

Flem's cheeks burned. "No need to worry about that, old buddy. I'm only permitted to write obituaries."

ꕥ

It had been another long day, and try as he may, Flem couldn't stop thinking about what Aldur had told him. The hardest part was keeping it from Liesel. She knew when he was holding something back. Weary, he switched off the lamp. But as soon as his head hit the pillow, the phone started ringing.

"Who's calling us at this hour?" Liesel asked.

"There's only one way to find out." Flem picked up the receiver.

"It's official! Marlene is with child!"

"She's pregnant?"

"Who's pregnant?" Liesel asked. "Who are you talking to?"

"Your brother," Flem whispered, kissing Liesel's cheek as she quietly squealed from her side of the bed.

"I meant to phone you after her appointment," Aldur explained, "but I was in a hurry to do some more digging at the office."

Flem switched on the lamp. "What did you find out?"

"Meet me for lunch tomorrow and I'll tell you."

"Where?" Flem asked.

"That café on Havnegrade, the one near the Ministry of Justice."

"What time?"

"Noon," Aldur said. "If I'm a few minutes late, wait for me."

"Shall we synchronize our watches?" Flem asked with a surge of adrenalin he hadn't felt since his days working with the Resistance.

"That won't be necessary…for now at least. Kiss my sister goodnight, and I'll see you tomorrow."

"All right, out with it!" Liesel demanded the instant he hung up.

"Out with what?"

"Whatever you and my brother are cooking up."

"We're having lunch," he said, turning off the lamp.

"What does Aldur want you to do?"

"This." Flem scooped her into his arms and kissed her.

"You don't play fair!" she complained when he finally let her go.

"Well, you asked what he wanted so I showed you instead."

"You really expect me to believe that?"

"He told me to kiss you goodnight. Now, hold me so I can fall asleep. I've got a busy day tomorrow."

"Well don't forget to synchronize your watch before your rendezvous," she said, tearing up.

"Come on, Liesel. We're only meeting for lunch. You've no need to cry."

"I'm your wife! So don't lie to me, Flem! You might as well turn the lamp on again, because neither of us is getting any sleep until you start telling me the truth."

"It's not what you think, min smukke."

"That's the problem. I don't know what to think."

"We just want to protect you."

"From what?"

"Fine!" Flem sat up in bed and switched the lamp on again. "I'll tell you, even though I promised Aldur I wouldn't. But I warn you, you're not going to like it, Liesel. You'll wish you'd never asked."

Three

Aldur smiled up at the new waitress. "I'll have your Øllebrød."

"Øllebrød at breakfast, not lunch!" she informed him in a thick Russian accent. Her body language called him an imbecile. "Have only what printed on menu."

Aldur restrained himself. "Bring me a sandwich and a lager then," he said as Flem walked through the door.

"Have many sandwich. Which you want?"

"Pick one!"

She plucked the menu out of his hand.

Aldur snatched it back. "If you don't mind, my friend still has to order."

"You tell friend order from menu, this menu, and I bring."

"What was that all about?" Flem asked with a wrinkled brow as he sat down at the table.

Aldur passed him the menu. "I haven't the slightest idea, but I know one thing."

"What's that?"

"Attitudes are contagious."

"I know, but forget about her. Tell me what you found out."

Aldur leaned forward and lowered his voice. "Two weeks before the war ended, the Resistance confiscated a list from Frits Clausen's house with all the names of Danish members of the Nazi Party."

"Was that the document you found in that file?"

"What I found was a mimeograph. The Court has the original. The judge ordered that it be kept under strict archival laws."

"Why?"

"Only sanctioned universities and genealogical associations will ever see it."

"I don't understand," Flem said.

"They're protecting themselves and their Nazi associates from reprisals, Flem."

"I can't believe it."

"They only care about Denmark's reputation, not justice. Since October of '43 we've been a shining star, and they don't want it tarnished by the dirty little fact most of our ranking officials were quislings."

"Even our justices?"

"Them too!" Aldur said, wanting to spit.

"Our courts are supposed to punish criminals."

"The world won't read a single name on the Bovrup Index until 2018," Aldur said, as the waitress approached their table. "By then, every quisling will be rotting in his grave."

"Ready order now?"

Flem handed her the menu. "Bring me whatever he's having."

"What do you intend to do?" Flem asked as she walked away.

Aldur shrugged. "Me? I'm just a glorified clerk."

"A clerk who works for the Ministry of Justice."

"Ministry of Injustice you mean. Honestly, Flem, if Marlene weren't pregnant, I'd be looking for another job."

"Does she know?" Flem asked.

"I couldn't keep it from her. She saw how upset I was."

Flem sighed. "I know what you mean. I couldn't either."

"You told Liesel?"

"After you called last night, I had no choice."

"How did she take it?"

"Not nearly as hard as I thought she would." Flem smiled. "After that fuss she made, I think she felt obligated. Your sister took it on the chin, but she felt betrayed. Who wouldn't? The myth of our heroism isn't easy to let go of."

"It wasn't all a myth, Flem. Many of our countrymen did the right thing and that deserves praise."

"What God did, you mean."

"Of course," Aldur agreed.

"That the Lord accomplished what He did, in spite of all our quislings, makes it an even greater miracle."

"They make me want to puke."

Flem smiled. "You're a moralist, old buddy, and I mean that in the best possible way. Even your short-lived enthrallment with the Nazis had an underpinning of what you saw as justice at the time."

Aldur rolled his eyes, embarrassed to even think about it.

"Not to mention a great cover for your work with the Resistance. It saved your tush on more than one occasion," Flem reminded him as the waitress returned with their platters.

She plunked them down on the table. "Anything else need?"

Aldur forced a smile to see if she'd return it, but her lips looked as if they'd been chiseled in granite. "We're good. Thank you."

They waited until she walked away, then Flem leaned across the table. "There is definitely something wrong with that woman."

Aldur nodded then lowered his head. "We thank you for our food, Lord, and bless the new waitress. She really needs it." After their amens, Aldur checked his watch. "Let's eat. I need to get back to the office."

"I have obituaries to write, and I promised to take Caleb to visit my folks this afternoon." Flem picked up his sandwich. "This chicken smells delicious."

"Don't!" Aldur exclaimed, his mouth filled with food.

"Don't what?" Flem asked.

Aldur raised his index finger as he gulped down some lager. "Don't eat that sandwich! It's not chicken."

ᘐᘔ

Sol Lund had just stuck Jacob's letter back in the envelope when he heard the front door open.

"Zayde? Zayde? Where are you?"

His grandson's angelic voice filled Sol's heart with joy. "I'm up here in the library," he said dropping the envelope on the table next to his chair. "I'll be down just as soon as I can get these arthritic knees to cooperate."

"Don't bother, Father," Flem called up the stairs. "We're on our way."

Twenty seconds later, Caleb dashed into the room and hopped onto his grandfather's lap. As Flem kissed Sol's bald spot, Caleb began rubbing his cheek against Sol's beard. Whiskers, of late, seemed to fascinate the child.

"Why don't you have a beard, Father?" Caleb asked Flem.

"I will one day, when I get old," he replied.

Sol gasped. "Did you hear that, Caleb? Your father just called me an old man."

"Aren't you, Zayde?"

Sol struggled not to laugh. "Well … perhaps. But just a little."

"Your grandfather started growing those whiskers last year. I think he got jealous of your Uncle Jacob's."

Caleb rubbed his own cheeks. "Will my face grow hairs when I'm old, Zayde?"

This time Sol gave into his mirth. "Only if you don't cut them, my boy, only if you don't cut them." Sol loved hearing his grandson call him Zayde. Not only did the Yiddish word for grandfather sound friendlier than the Danish bedstefar, but it brought back many treasured memories.

"Is that a letter from Jacob?" Flem picked up the envelope. "Mind if I read it?"

"Why not? I've already read it twice."

"It was that good?" Flem said.

"The second time was between the lines."

"What do you mean?" Flem asked.

"Read it for yourself then we'll talk," Sol told him as his niece, Inger, entered the library flashing young Caleb a smile.

The boy scrambled off Sol's lap and into Inger's arms, screeching with joy.

Flem smiled. "I'll go downstairs to read. It's quieter there."

"Well, make sure you read it twice!" Sol reminded him.

ꙮ

As Flem slid the letter into its envelope, his thoughts took him back to the night Katlev finally unburdened himself about Sima's fatal accident, an accident for which the old man held himself solely responsible. Even now, Flem could see the pain in Katlev's eyes as he pleaded with him to never make his mistake, to never run away from God and His purpose.

Flem removed the letter from its envelope again. This time he would read what Jacob wrote slowly…and between the lines.

Four

Preparing to pray the Amidah, Jacob donned his tallit with his face set toward where the Holy Temple once stood. When he reached the fifteenth Birkat, the blessing which petitioned the Branch of David to arise and bring salvation to Israel, Jacob prayed intimately for he knew the Messiah, knew Him by name, Yeshua. It was the name Gabriel gave to Miriam, the name that declared Yeshua's mission to save His people Israel. As soon as Jacob finished praying the nineteenth blessing, he returned to the main house. Obeying the Messiah's instructions, he picked up the receiver and clicked for the operator.

"Yes, please. I wish to place a person-to-person call to Fleming Lund in Copenhagen, Denmark."

ஐ

Devorah entered the parlor toting a silver platter filled with triangular cookies. "I know it's not Purim," she told Jacob, "but I thought I'd surprise you and Mati with my Hamantaschen." The aroma of her apricot, date, and poppy seed pastries made Jacob's mouth water. They were named for Haman, the villain the Persian king had ordered to be hung by the neck until dead…and on the very same gallows Haman had erected to hang all of Persia's Jews on.

"Matityahu is a blessed man," Jacob told her as her husband thundered into the parlor with stormy eyes.

"Those Edomites," Matityahu yelled, his favorite epitaph these days for the British, "have gone and done it again!"

Devorah set her tray down on the table. "Now remember your blood pressure, Mati!"

"They have no sense of justice!" Matityahu continued, paying her no mind.

"But God is still in control," she reminded him, "so calm down."

She led him to his favorite chair and placed his feet up on the hassock. Jacob scooted to the far end of the sofa to be closer to his friend. "What happened?"

"Arabs! Outside Jaffa Gate! They ambushed one of our buses and mowed down eight Jews."

Jacob's heart broke.

"And guess who those Edomites arrested? Thirteen members of Irgun's Zvai Leumi."

"Why?" Jacob asked.

"They were armed! Arabs alone can possess guns and ammunition. Never mind Hajj Amin el Husseini's threats to annihilate every last one of us."

Jacob shut his eyes. Matityahu spoke the truth. The Mufti of Jerusalem had sworn on more than one occasion not to rest until every Jew in Palestine had been driven into the sea.

"We have a promise from the Most High," Jacob started to remind him when a ring from the telephone grabbed his attention.

"Shalom…yes, he's here. I'll put him on," Devorah said. "It's for you, Jacob. Fleming Lund…he's returning your call."

ᘓᘏ

"Your party is on the line. Go ahead."

"Fleming? Are you there?"

"I am," Flem said. "It's so good to hear your voice again. Are you well, Jacob?"

"Remarkably so, thank you…except when I try to sleep."

Flem glanced at Liesel. "You're not sleeping well, Jacob?"

"You and your family have been invading my dreams for several weeks now."

Flem relaxed. "You've been dreaming about us?"

"And it's always the same dream, or a version of it. You're here… in the Land."

"In Palestine? Really?"

"So is your family … only not exactly here but somewhere close by. You're helping the Aliyah Beit. Do you know who they are, Fleming?"

"Of course! What Jew doesn't?"

"Adonai is using you again."

Flem's heart began to race.

"Only this time, Fleming, you're not smuggling our people to safety in some foreign land. You're returning them here, to our land."

Flem's heart pounded as he struggled to find words.

"You must pray, Fleming!" Jacob told him after several seconds of silence. "You must ask Yeshua where it is that He wants you, there in Denmark or over here."

"What's Jacob saying?" Liesel asked. "You look so strange."

"I will, Jacob," Flem said, ignoring her. "I promise."

"Good! Then I will say shalom for now, but give my love to your family, especially your dear father. We've been writing to each other on a regular basis."

"I will," Flem said neglecting to mention that he'd read Jacob's latest letter earlier that afternoon. It would've kept them on the line longer, and from Liesel's expression, Flem knew his wife was chomping at the bit to give him what his father's detective novels referred to as the third-degree.

"Just send me a telegram, Fleming. These person-to-person calls are costly, and you have a growing family to support."

"I will, Jacob, just as soon as I hear from the Lord. Shalom! Stay safe over there! You're in our prayers, too."

"What did Jacob want?" Liesel asked the second Flem hung up the receiver.

"He just wants me to pray about something," Flem said, trying not to sound annoyed by her question.

"Pray about what?"

"Some dreams he's been having."

"About us?"

"He just misses us, min smukke. We're all the family he has now, except for the Goldbergs, of course."

"Katlev bequeathed us to him, I know, and I'm glad that he did, but I'm not glad that you're doing it again."

"Doing what again?"

"You're holding something back. Don't deny it. I hear it in your voice."

Flem smiled and kissed her cheek. "You know me too well, Liesel, you always have."

"Is that bad?"

"No, it's not bad, but disconcerting at times."

"Like now?" she persisted with a determined glint in her eyes.

"Please, min smukke, just give me a few days to pray about this. Okay? Then I promise I'll tell you everything."

Caleb tugged at Flem's pantleg. "Will you tell me too, Father?"

He smiled down at the boy. "Of course, right after I tell your mother."

"Yes, Father, but…"

"But what, Caleb?"

"Don't tell her with more words than you tell me, okay?"

Five

After reading about forty-two Jewish Holocaust survivors who were brutally murdered when they returned to their homes in Poland, Juhl's eyes felt weighty, but not as heavy as his heart.

"Will you please turn out that lamp? We need to get some sleep!" Deidre plucked the magazine he'd been reading out of his hands and tossed it across the room.

He turned off the lamp. "I doubt I can after what I just read."

"Then don't read distressing news before bed, not with your work schedule. What you need, what we both need, is a vacation."

Juhl perked up. His dear wife had just opened the door he'd been wanting to walk through for a week. "You're so right, Yndling! We do need a vacation … a nice long vacation."

"What do you have in mind?" she asked, rolling over to face him.

Juhl's heart began to race. "Somewhere warm, much warmer than here, an island in the Mediterranean near Greece, with glimmering sand and brilliant sunshine."

"Oh, Juhl, that sounds glorious. Only do you think the hospital will give you that much time off?"

Juhl swallowed hard before answering. "They won't need to, Yndling. This won't be a vacation for me."

Deidre sat up in bed and just stared at him.

Juhl switched the lamp on again. "Just hear me out, Deidre."

"Not with that look in your eye! I know it all too well!"

"I've been offered a position at a Displaced Persons Hospital in Cyprus."

"You can't do this to me again, Juhl! Not again!"

"But, Deidre, those poor souls need medical attention. Without good care they won't survive."

"But why must it be you? Haven't you done enough already?"

"Those camps aren't much better than the ones the Jews were liberated from."

"I get that, Juhl. Only, let some other doctor do it. You were nearly killed working for the Resistance. Besides, we're not even Jewish."

"No, but our son-in-law is," Juhl reminded her harshly.

"You're not being fair, Juhl!"

"I don't have to be fair or Jewish! I'm a doctor, Deidre. That's enough. And I've been offered a job."

"Offered?"

"I made a few inquiries," he said, moderating his tone. "The point is, there's a position that needs to be filled in Nicosia…and it's sixty degrees there in December. Can't you at least pray about it, Deidre?" When she stared back in silence, Juhl took her hands. "I'm sorry I got so frustrated. I shouldn't have, not after all you endured because of my work in the Resistance, but please, will you just take it to the Lord before you give me your answer?"

ꙮ

Having slept deeply and without dreaming, Jacob jumped out of bed. As he headed for the latrine, he felt young again, like a man in his thirties. Then Jacob remembered the expression in Matityahu's eyes when he told him about the ambush and again felt his age. He washed and dressed but even the anticipation of having Flem and his family living close by couldn't lighten his heart as he crossed the walkway to the main house.

"Boker tov," Devorah greeted him, cheery as ever.

"Good morning to you, too," he said forcing a smile and feeling like a liar.

"Mati should be in in a few minutes if he doesn't get sidetracked. He's out feeding the chickens."

Her breakfast array—yogurt, hard cheese, omelets, flatbread, and fresh butter—looked delicious. But Jacob had no appetite for it this morning. "One would think you were cooking for an army."

"It's the morning spread of the kibbutz we spent the first five years of our marriage on."

"Back in the twenties, I know … you've told me before."

Devorah eyed him shrewdly. "What's wrong with you, Jacob? Did those dreams of yours rob you of sleep again?"

"I had no dreams last night."

"Then why are you out of sorts?" She set a glass of juice next to his plate. "Your spirits were high after talking to Fleming. So, what's troubling you now?"

"That ambush! I can't stop thinking about it."

"Well, ruminating won't change anything. Take your thoughts captive. Say the blessing and eat!"

Jacob sighed, knowing she was right. He said the blessing over the food then took his seat and scooped one of her omelets onto his plate. "I just don't understand why they won't let us protect ourselves."

"The Arabs won't like it. That's why."

"But this is our land. Elohim gave it to us."

"They don't see it that way."

"They claim to be a Christian nation! Don't they read prophecy?"

Devorah smiled wryly. "They read it, just not the way we do, Jacob."

"Well, they should!"

"The Christian Church, they've been taught, has replaced us as God's chosen people."

"Lies, no matter how fervently they're believed, cannot—will not—change what Adonai has declared in His Word, that Israel will be regathered, and the Kingdom restored."

"But when, Jacob?" Devorah asked, refilling her coffee. "Each one of those British White Papers makes matters here worse for us."

Again, Jacob knew she was right. He picked up his fork and broke off a piece of his omelet, but he was unable to bring it to his mouth. "Whether they know it or not, they're turning what could have been a blessing into a curse. Why can't they see it?"

Devorah sat down next to him. "They don't want to, Jacob. It's as simple as that. They have an agenda and the Arabs, not us Jews, are in a position to aid its fulfillment."

"But every English monarch coronated over the last thousand years took an oath on the Bible, a Bible filled, I might add, with prophecies about Israel's restoration."

"They want oil, and the Arabs have plenty of it."

Jacob dropped his fork on his plate, stood and shoved his chair back under the table. "Then they are idol worshipers!"

"Where are you going?"

"To read the Scriptures."

Devorah shrugged. "Then go back to your room, Jacob, if it'll make you feel better. I'll keep everything warm for you."

"You're most gracious, Devorah. But you've no need to. I won't be back for hours. I'm going to Jaffa Gate."

Color drained from Devorah's cheeks. "Why?"

"To declare Elohim's Word to those Edomites!" Jacob said, borrowing Matityahu's slur for the British Mandate government administrators in Palestine. "They need to know whom it is that they're thwarting. It's not us Jews, Devorah. It's Elohim!"

Six

As Jacob trod the dusty streets of the Old City wrapped in his prayer shawl, he imagined beholding the glory of King Solomon's Temple when Jerusalem was a fortress surrounded on all sides except one by great ravines that dropped 650 feet, forming a vast chasm. Only on the northwest border did the City of God connect with the mainland. Even at twilight the Temple had glittered like gold.

But as Jacob grew nearer to Jaffa Gate, the only thing glittering was the dome of that abomination the world knew as the Al-Aqsa Mosque. Four laughing British soldiers stood outside the Gate as several Arbs and a handful of Bedouins passed through the entrance into the north-west quadrant, the second largest section of old Jerusalem, known as the Christian quarter. Arabs controlled the largest area, Armenians the third. The British Mandate government, naturally, assigned the smallest quarter to the Jews.

Knowing he must fulfill what he came there to do, Jacob pulled his tallit up over his head. "Fill my mouth with Your words," he prayed under his breath, "and I shall declare them!"

ꕥ

Flem folded his tallit. Disappointed at getting no answer from the Lord regarding Jacob's dreams, he placed it in the drawer next to his kippah.

"Father! Father! Let me in. Something terrible has happened!"

When Flem opened the door, his son's cheeks were ruddy. "What is it, Caleb? What's wrong?"

"Floxy won't move!"

"Where's your mother?" Flem asked.

"With Mrs. Sorensen," the child said as tears streamed from his eyes. "Hurry, Father! Please!"

Fearing the worst, Flem hoisted his son on his hip. "Where is he?" he asked as he ran down the stairs holding the boy tightly.

"In front of the ice box."

The moment they entered the kitchen, Flem could tell that their kitty was dead. "Go get your mother," Flem told him, rummaging through a drawer for an older dish towel, one he could use to wrap the poor creature in for burial.

Liesel rushed in a few minutes later.

"Where's Caleb?" Flem asked her.

"I told him to stay with Mrs. Sorensen. I'll telephone Aldur and let him know."

"Do you want to tell Caleb or shall I?" Flem asked her.

"Tell him? He's the one who told me."

"Your cat had a good life, min smukke, a good, long life." Flem took her hands. "There's a time to live and time to die."

"And a time to grieve!" she said, snatching them back again. "So, spare me the eulogy!"

"What did I say wrong?" he asked.

"Floxy was *our* cat...or so I thought!"

"He was! I loved that cat. Why, if it weren't for him, we wouldn't be married now."

"What's that supposed to mean?"

"Don't you remember? You were looking for Floxy when you overheard my mother's tirade and ran over to warn us about Aldur."

Liesel finally smiled, but weakly.

Flem pulled out his handkerchief to dry her tears. "Am I forgiven?"

ℵ

Steven Greenbaum opened his desk, removed the yellowed *New York Times* clipping dated five months ago, and read it aloud for the umpteenth time. "British White Paper Links Jewish Agency to Zionist Terrorism in Palestine."

It was this article that spurred him to pressure his well-connected old man to pull the necessary strings to get him admitted to Hebrew University. His real agenda and childhood dream of joining the Aliyah Beit, he kept secret.

When the door opened then slammed shut again, his trip down memory lane ended.

"They've called another meeting," Bucky said making a beeline for the tuna sandwiches on the credenza. "So, pack your bags! They want us in Baltimore by the end of this week."

"What do you mean 'us'?" Steven asked him. "I only got here five months ago."

Bucky shrugged, then chomped into his sandwich.

"What do I tell my dad? I'm supposed to be going to school."

"Your family lives on Long Island. How will they know if you don't tell them?"

"What if I run into someone?"

Bucky made a face. "In Baltimore?"

"Stranger things have happened!" Steven said.

Bucky reached for a tumbler. "Look, the worst that can happen, and probably won't, is they'll cut you off."

"But I need the dough!"

"You're a big boy now, Stevie. It's time you learned to make do like the rest of us slobs."

Steven took a deep breath to stop from saying what he wanted to, then asked. "What time are they picking us up?"

ℵ

When two Catholic priests exited Jaffa Gate, Jacob knew he could no longer delay what he'd come there to do. "You claim to know God, but you continually thwart His plans!"

All around him heads turned.

"'Behold, the days are coming when it will no longer be said as Adonai lives who brought up the sons of Israel out of Egypt but as Adonai lives who brought the sons of Israel out of the land of the north and all the lands where I've driven them. I will bring them again into the land I gave their fathers. Although I sent them far off among the nations and scattered them among the lands, I was a sanctuary to them in the countries where they went… I shall again gather them from all the nations, assemble them out of the lands in which I scattered them, and I shall give them the land of Israel!' "

Then a stone struck Jacob's brow. He staggered backwards but quickly regained his balance.

"You're causing a disturbance here," a British officer yelled, running up to him. "Go on home and take care of that gash before something worse happens to you."

"Is that a threat?" Jacob asked as a trickle of warm blood moistened his eyebrow.

"I can't have you out here causing a commotion."

"Is it illegal now for a Jew to quote Scripture in the Holy Land?"

"Why stir up trouble? Be a good chap and move along. Don't force me to run you in."

"What about that Arab who struck me? Will you run him in, too?" Jacob asked as another rock stuck him, this time in the gut. It propelled Jacob backwards. His skull collided with the cobblestones and the world faded.

ꕥ

Floxy's burial went as well as could be expected. Flem glanced at his watch. "I need to hurry. I'm late," he told Liesel as they rounded the side of the house to the front porch.

"Is Floxy in heaven?" Caleb asked when his father opened the front door.

"Well?" Liesel said, smiling. "Our son asked you a question."

"He asked both of us, min smukke. Ladies before gentlemen."

"Aren't husbands accountable to God as the spiritual High Priest of their home?"

"Katlev warned me about you," Flem teased, returning her smile.

"What do you mean?" she asked.

"He said I'll need to stay on my toes with you for my wife, and now I understand why."

Caleb folded his arms. "You're doing it again!"

"Doing what?" Flem asked.

"Talking to my mother and not answering my question."

"You're right. I apologize. But you'll have to wait till I get back. I'm already late as it is."

"Because you talk to her with too many words."

Liesel covered her mouth, but Flem saw her smile. "And why is that?" he asked.

"Cause you love her…"

"That's right! And when you get a little older," Flem said, stooping to look in his son's eyes, "I'll use even more words with you, hundreds of them."

Caleb hung his head.

"Now what's the matter?" Flem asked.

"I can only count to ten."

ꕥ

"It's about time you got here!" Geørg Drøhse, the editor-in-chief of the *Copenhagen Gazette*, frowned as Flem hung up his coat.

"My son had an emergency this morning."

"Is the boy okay?"

"Our cat died," Flem explained.

"Well, a train ran the tracks forty-five minutes ago coming in from Østerport. I need you to get over there and write it up."

"Me? What about Müller?"

"He's no longer with us… Well? Do you want the assignment or don't you?"

"Absolutely!" Flem said.

"Then get going! I'll need your copy on my desk by three, and not a second later, if you intend to keep Müller's beat."

"I do! And it will be," Flem assured him. "It's a promise!"

ጀጋ

"I don't like it!" Devorah said. "Jacob should've been back by now. Please go and look for him, Mati."

"You worry too much, woman," he told her as he washed his hands at the kitchen sink.

"But he didn't eat a morsel this morning."

"Look, Jacob survived Theresienstadt, didn't he? Missing a meal now and then isn't going to kill him."

Devorah held out a hand towel. "That's not what I'm worried about, Mati. I told you what he intended to do."

Matityahu sighed then glanced at his wristwatch. "If he's not back by two, I'll go. Now let's have our lunch."

"Two is too late. It'll be Shabbos in a few more hours."

Matityahu sighed. Dissuading his wife once she'd made up her mind was next to impossible. "Fine! I'll go now," he said, handing her back the towel.

She smiled. "Thank you, Mati! You're a dear!"

"Sure, sure! Only, thank me with something more substantial than words, something I can eat on the way so I don't starve."

Seven

A passenger train leaving Østerport, bound for Copenhagen derailed at 9:46 a.m. this morning. While this accident, Flem typed, is still under investigation, some officials now believe that a signalman's error may have caused the derailment. Six lost their lives. One is in critical condition. The fifteen who were injured are in stable condition and expected to be discharged from Bispebjerg Hospital within two days. Names of the deceased are being held pending notification of their next of kin.

Gut still in knots, Flem ripped the shortest—and the most painful—copy he'd ever pounded out from the typewriter.

How he'd ever find the right words to break the terrible news to Aldur, Liesel, and his in-laws, he didn't know. All he knew now was that he had to get out of there…had to pray.

With his head tucked to avoid making eye contact, lest someone ask him what was wrong, Flem hurried into Geørg's office. Relieved to find the boss's chair empty, he laid his copy on Geørg's blotter and made a hasty retreat. Outside, snow clouds, the first Copenhagen had seen in over a week, darkened the sky. Flem rushed to his car and opened the door. As he slid behind the wheel, he got an idea. If he could pull it off, it would spare him being the bearer of bad news more than once.

He checked his watch. Except for the challah bread, Liesel probably wouldn't have started dinner yet—and if she had, she could always add enough for five more.

ᘓᘐ

Matityahu returned home. Greeting the Sabbath with joy would be difficult, as difficult as telling Devorah he'd failed in his mission. Finding the dining room table still unset, he hastened to the kitchen. It was empty, too. Then he detected the aroma of her freshly baked bread.

He glanced over at the baker's rack where two loaves of her braided challah sat cooling. On the stove were three pots, and they all had lids.

She must've gone outside to feed his hens. He rushed out back only to be disappointed. His chickens clucked about his feet demanding to be fed. Where could the woman be? This just wasn't like her. He hurried into the shed praying, grabbed a bag of feed and scattered it around. When he finished, he'd intended to start calling Devorah's friends, but hearing what sounded like an engine, he ran to the front of the house. An armor-plated, 2.5-ton Hagenah truck pulled to a stop. Then, its double doors opened. An attractive young nurse jumped out, then turned around and offered her hand to Devorah.

Flooded with relief, Matityahu ran over to greet them. "I've been so worried! Where have you been?"

"Mati, dear, I want you should meet Julie Abercrombie."

Matityahu flashed her a perfunctory smile then turned back to Devorah. "You scared the life out of me! Couldn't you at least have left me a note?"

"You'll never guess who she is, Mati."

"She is obviously a nurse!" he said.

"Mati, Mati, try to focus! I said *who* she is, not *what*!"

When a young British officer and a sabra jumped out of the truck,

Matityahu addressed the Brit. "Since my wife prefers playing word games, will you kindly tell me what's going on?"

The young officer smiled warmly. "Your friend Jacob is in the hospital … and will be for the next few days. But he's expected to recover."

"What happened?" Matityahu asked in a more respectful tone.

"Some Arab threw a rock at him. He fell and hit his head."

"Jacob was unconscious when they brought him in. Julie was the charge nurse," his wife explained excitedly.

"Perhaps I should take it from here," the nurse suggested.

"Good idea! Only, let's go inside so I can finish preparing our dinner." Devorah turned to her husband. "We're having guests for Shabbat, Mati."

Matityahu groaned.

"Oh, shush! When the pieces come together, I promise you, Mati, you'll be delighted."

"It's not that," he said, "I'm delighted now."

"Well, you have a strange way of showing it, Mati dear."

"I'm embarrassed, that's all!"

Everyone else smiled.

When they reached the parlor, all except Devorah took a seat. "Go ahead, Julie, tell my husband who you are. I want to see his expression before I go."

"Do you remember hearing about a retired army doctor, a Scottish missionary named Abercrombie who treated Sima?"

Gooseflesh pricked Matityahu's arms.

Julie smiled. "He was our grandfather. This is my brother, Captain Roger Abercrombie."

Matityahu extended his hand. "I'm truly honored to meet you, both of you."

"And I'm Julie's boyfriend, Asher Zelenko," the sabra explained. "Thanks for inviting us to share your Shabbos."

"We're honored to have you, all three of you," Matityahu said. "I'm just sorry Jacob couldn't be here to celebrate with us."

"I better get back to the kitchen and get busy. It'll be dark soon."

"Can I help you?" Julie asked.

"No, dear. You're needed right where you are."

"My wife works faster when there is no one to talk to. Now tell me, how did you manage to find us?"

"Jacob kept whispering Yeshua's name when he came to," Julie said. "So, I asked him if he knew of a rabbi named Matityahu Goldberg. When I found out that he lived with you I immediately phoned Roger."

"We went to that kibbutz you used to live on when we first got stationed here," Roger explained. "But those who remembered you didn't know where you'd moved to, so we gave up our search. When Julie phoned me about Jacob, I begged Asher to pick you up and bring you to the hospital."

"Only, you'd already left when I got here," Asher explained. "So, I brought your wife instead."

"Are you a believer, too?" Matityahu inquired, suspecting that he might be.

"A believer in what?" Asher asked.

Julie laughed. "Matityahu wants to know about your relationship with the Lord."

"Ah! You want to know what I think of Yeshua, eh?"

Asher's use of the Messiah's Hebrew name, and not the acronym Yeshu which meant "may his name and memory be blotted out," brought a smile to Matityahu's lips. "I suspected you might be one of us!"

"There are others as well," Asher assured him.

"They're a rather hush-hush group," Roger added. "You might say an underground synagogue."

Asher grinned. "What about you and your wife? Are you covert as well?"

Matityahu shrugged. "Let's just say we've learned over the years whom not to cast our pearls before. But when the Ruach prompts us, we plant seeds then ask questions that we hope will make them think seriously about certain matters. With truth-seekers we're less cryptic."

"What about you and Devorah?" Julie asked. "Do you have other believers you can worship with?"

"A few, but not a full minion," Matityahu said sadly. "So, we go to synagogue. What about you, Asher?"

"We have a minion when everyone shows up. Julie and I were supposed to join them tonight until Adonai changed our plans."

"Well, we're delighted the Lord did," Matityahu told him.

"Many of our people fleeing Europe, both before and after the war, no longer believe in God at all, not a loving one anyway. And after two thousand years of persecution, most Jews are a bit leery of Christians. I was fortunate, however. My grandparents escaped Russia with their faith intact. So, when Julie started pointing out some of the Messianic prophecies that line up with Yeshua, I studied it out."

Roger laughed. "Now, Asher, tell the truth, the whole truth! My sister's charms inspired your research!"

Asher looked at Julie and smiled. "Let's just say that your sister's beauty, both inside and out, didn't impede it."

Matityahu chuckled. "My motive wasn't any purer than yours, Asher. So don't let that bother you. I simply wanted to prove Sima wrong! So, you see, the Messiah has been gracious to both of us."

When the phone began to ring, Matityahu got up and answered it. "Shalom…Yes…of course." He glanced over at Asher, then held out the receiver. "It's for you."

Looking tense, Asher said, "Shalom…Yes. Oh, I see…of course." He checked his watch. "I'll be there in fifteen minutes."

"What is it? What's wrong?" Julie asked, rushing over to him as he hung up the phone.

"Arabs are attacking a settlement south of here. I have to go."

"Of course," Roger told him. "I'll have one of our friends take us back. Go on. You need to get out of here."

Julie walked him to the door and kissed him. "Be careful. And call me as soon as you can. We'll be praying."

"All of us," Matityahu affirmed.

ꕥ

"Of course, I'd love to have everyone over for Shabbat." Liesel glanced up at the clock. "But these things take planning. Why didn't you tell me sooner?"

"There wasn't time, min smukke. I got the idea on the way home. But don't worry," Flem said, "I'll call everyone if you'll phone Aldur."

"No, min smukke!" Liesel lifted the receiver and handed it to him. "You'll call all of them, including my brother. I have a dinner to prepare for six more mouths."

Only five, Flem corrected her silently.

"And less than three hours to do it."

Confused because Marlene still wasn't home, even though she'd asked him to leave work earlier than usual so they could start their long weekend together, Aldur searched the apartment a second time for a note.

When the phone started ringing, he grabbed it. "Where are you? I've been worried crazy!"

After a few seconds of silence, Flem said, "It's me, Aldur. We'd like to have you over for dinner tonight. Your folks will be here as well, mine too."

"I'll have to check with Marlene first…if she ever gets back."

"No, you don't, I mean, well, I saw her earlier today."

"You did? That's strange. She never phoned to let me know…we sort of had plans for tonight."

"She must not have had time."

"Well, if that's what she wants, we'll leave as soon as she gets back."

"There's no need to wait, Aldur. It's all been arranged."

Aldur shrugged. Oh well, at least he didn't have to worry about why Marlene wasn't home. "Okay then. I'll be over as soon as I shower and change clothes."

ꕥ

Flem stared at Liesel's elegantly set Sabbath table that had one lone empty chair. Thankfully, Mrs. Sorensen had agreed to let Caleb spend the night, but the sun was close to setting and he was eager to get this ordeal over with. He turned to Liesel. "We need to get started."

"How can we? Marlene's still not here."

"But the Sabbath is," he reminded her gently, praying she'd give in without a fight.

With a forced smile, she turned to her guests. "Excuse me, everyone. It's time for us to greet the Sabbath."

She lit the candles.

As Flem blessed Adonai for the wine and the bread, Aldur checked his watch. No longer able to keep up the pretense, Flem turned to address his guests. "Before we go any further, there's something I have to tell you… all of you. It's the reason, the real reason, I wanted us all to be together tonight."

Flem's somber tone elicited murmurs around the table.

"Our lead journalist resigned today. So Geørg sent me out to cover the train derailment that I'm sure all of you must've heard about by now." Flem watched as the expression in his brother-in-law's eyes turned to dread and color drained from his face.

He jumped up, nearly knocking over his chair. "Is my wife dead?"

Feeling sick, Flem nodded slowly.

As everyone around the table gasped, Aldur bolted from the room.

Flem started to go after him.

Liesel grabbed his arm. "I'll see to my brother. Take care of my parents."

ꕥ

When Liesel reached the parlor, she froze. Aldur had his back to her, staring stoically out the window. What could she say to him?

Hearing a still, small voice tell her to just listen, she walked over and opened her arms. Aldur dove into them. For a long time neither of them spoke.

"Marlene had morning sickness again when she got up."

Liesel comforted him, but only with her eyes.

"Before she left, do you know what she told me?"

Liesel shook her head.

"That she hoped it would be her last."

Not knowing what to say, she rubbed his arms. "Why don't we sit on the sofa?"

He agreed.

Liesel switched on the lamp then waited until he was ready to speak.

"Would you mind taking that yellow layette set that Marline bought for the baby the next time you come over? Give it to whoever needs it. I can't bear looking at it again."

"Of course," Liesel assured him.

"All day I've sensed something was wrong. It got heavier when Flem told me he'd seen Marlene earlier."

"I'm sure Flem meant well," Liesel said, wanting to strangle her husband.

"At first I attributed it to Floxy dying, but while I was looking out the window I realized the Lord was preparing me for this all day."

"Preparing you? How?"

Aldur twisted his wedding band. "Remember that day when I overheard Flem's prayer and ran out of the chapel? I hated Father or thought I did. Mother accused me of losing my soul. She said I wasn't her son, not the one she raised. Worst of all," he said looking at Liesel, "you were in the hospital because of me."

"It was an accident, Aldur. You weren't responsible."

"An accident that never would've happened if I'd just stayed and listened to you."

"Then you would've heard Flem praying. Don't you see, Aldur? The Lord used my accident to change your heart. That's what's important."

"I know," Aldur said as tears welled in his eyes.

"Then you're not angry?"

"At the Lord? What good would that do? I can't, I won't, go back to living in darkness again. I have to trust. What else can I do?"

Loving her brother's heart, Liesel threw her arms around him. "He'll see us through this, Aldur. I know He will."

"That's what I'm counting on, Sis."

"Then let's go back in." Liesel stood, took his hands and pulled him up. "Our parents need us."

ꕥ

The men took their wine and conversation into the parlor while Devorah stacked dishes into the sink. "Tonight's been truly wonderful," she told Julie with a happy heart.

"Except for Asher being called away, it's been perfect. We're so thrilled to have finally found the two of you, regardless of how it happened."

Devorah rolled her eyes. "I knew there'd be trouble when Jacob told me what he intended to do."

"Intended to do?"

"Jacob didn't tell you?"

"Tell me what?"

Devorah shut off the faucet. "He was furious about last night's ambush and the injustice of not allowing Jews to own firearms."

Julie hung her head. "Guns only make matters worse. They can't cure hate."

Devorah stared at Julie. "How can matters get worse? Arabs have been attacking our settlements for decades. In 1929, they slaughtered not just us Jews, but their own people, anyone sympathetic to our plight. And what did your government do? They stood by and let it happen. No, Julie. I'm sorry, but I find very little difference between Hitler's policies and those of the British Mandate."

When Julie's eyes filled with tears, Devorah immediately regretted her outburst. "Forgive me, child," she said, leading Julie to a chair to sit down. "I shouldn't have taken my frustration out on you, especially not on the Sabbath."

"It's okay. You're right. My brother knows it, too, but we're caught in the middle."

Roger rushed into the kitchen. "What's wrong? Why are you crying?"

"I'm just worried about Asher."

"It's my fault," Devorah confessed as Matityahu joined them. "I made some comments that I shouldn't have."

"No, Devorah," Julie corrected her as someone knocked at the front door. "You were right. Our government does discriminate."

"That must be Mike," Roger said. "We need to get going. I don't want to make him late."

Devorah and Mati walked them to the front of the house. When Mati opened the door, a stone-faced lieutenant saluted Roger. "I'm here to take you and your sister back to the base, sir."

"What happened to Mike?" Roger asked.

"His unit was deployed to put down an uprising just south of here."

"That must be the same place the Hagenah sent Asher," Devorah said, clasping her throat.

"How bad is it?" Julie asked.

"It's not good, miss. They used explosives this time. So we won't know the actual death toll until morning."

༄༅

Deidre's heart broke for her son. "I wish there was something we could do to help ease your pain."

"Only God can do that, Mother."

"I know, but you shouldn't be alone, not tonight. Why don't you come home with us, Son?"

"I was hoping you'd ask," he said, surprising her.

"I was about to suggest that myself," Juhl said, breaking away from his conversation with Sol. "And not just for tonight."

"We'll see," Aldur said. "But I need to go back and pack some clothes."

"Not tonight you won't," Juhl said. "You can wear a pair of my pajamas and borrow anything else you need."

"Thanks, Dad. The truth is I'm not ready to face Marlene's belongings yet."

"Flem and I can go with you," Liesel offered.

"It's your Sabbath. You should rest," Deidre told her. "Juhl and I can manage. Can't we, Juhl?"

"It's the Lord's Sabbath, Mother," Aldur corrected her. "We should all rest tomorrow. By Sunday I'm sure I'll be up to managing it myself. There are some old photographs of Marlene's parents that I want to mail to her aunt. As far as I know, she's the only relative of Marlene who is still living."

"Well, let us know if there is anything we can do," Sol offered.

"There's really nothing you can do but there is something that all of you should know."

"What's that?" his father asked.

"I'm giving notice on Monday."

"Why?" his parents asked in unison.

"I thought you loved working there," his father added with a look of surprise.

"I did, but not anymore."

"Are you having a problem with one of your co-workers?" Deidre persisted.

"One? All of them, more likely…it's too soon to tell."

"What's that supposed to mean?"

"Let it go, Mother," Liesel warned her.

Deidre turned to her daughter. "You know about this?"

"She does, Mother. So does Flem. He was the first one I told."

"And you couldn't tell your own parents?"

Juhl placed his hand over hers. "When our son wants to tell us, he will. Let it go, Deidre."

Tears filled her eyes. "But I only want to help!"

"Well, you can't, Mother. Not this time, unless you can find me a job somewhere else."

"I'm sure I can at the hospital," Juhl said. "Our business office is hiring."

"Thanks, Dad. But that won't be far enough. I plan to leave Denmark."

"Leave Denmark!" Deidre said, horrified.

"Let it go, Mother," Liesel warned her for the second time.

Sol stood up. "This young man has just lost his wife and his child. Please! Can't he have a little peace on the Sabbath?"

"Sit down, Sol," Nettie whispered, tugging at his hand.

Deidre swiped away her tears. "I want to help."

"I know you do, Mother, but you can't."

"Yes, I can!" Deidre insisted, then turned to her husband. "Go on, tell him, Juhl!"

He stared back at her in silence that stilled everyone in the room. "Are you sure? Have you prayed this through?"

Deidre nodded. "It's what the Lord wants. I didn't…not at first... but now I do, Juhl. So, tell him."

"I've been offered a position at a hospital in the Mediterranean. A Displaced Persons hospital in Cyprus."

For several seconds Aldur said nothing. But Deidre could see that he was processing all the possibilities.

"How soon will you be leaving?" he finally asked.

"I need to be there before the end of next month."

Deidre touched her son's hand. "It's sixty degrees there in December. Warm sun and white sand is just the change you need. What do you say? Would you like to go with us, Aldur?"

Nine

Unable to bear another second of her husband's rhythmic breathing, Liesel crawled out of bed. She shoved her feet into her slippers, grabbed her robe, and hurried down the stairs to the kitchen. As a child, from bad dreams to bellyaches, warm milk always soothed her. Only, this particular nightmare wouldn't be that easy to wake up from. Marlene and her unborn child were dead. And now, making matters even worse, Aldur and her folks were planning to abandon her.

"What's wrong?" Flem asked, sneaking up behind her. "Couldn't you sleep?"

"Obviously not," she snapped, in no mood to be comforted, at least not by him.

"So, you decided to scald milk instead?" He smiled, nodding toward the stove. Seeing the milk boiling over, she burst into tears.

Flem turned off the burner then pulled her into his arms. "Why are you crying over spilt milk?"

She pulled away. "You're not funny!"

"What's wrong?"

"Why don't you tell me?" she demanded.

"I'm not the one crying."

"No! You're the one keeping secrets! Again!"

"What are you talking about?" he asked.

"Why didn't you tell me about Marlene? How do you think I felt, hearing about it with all the others?"

"I didn't do it to slight you. I only wanted everyone all together so I'd only have to make the announcement once."

"Well, I'm not everyone! I'm your wife, Flem!"

"You're right. I should have told you first. I really am sorry, min smukke." He lifted her chin and brushed away her tears.

But Liesel wasn't ready to be placated. "If that's true, then tell me. What does Jacob want you to pray about?"

Flem's heavy sigh fanned Liesel's frustrations.

"Is it that hard to confide in me?"

"No. I just haven't gotten an answer yet. Maybe we should pray about this together?"

"How can we? You won't tell me what we're praying for!"

"For God's will to be done!" Flem said, flaring at her indignation.

"Was it His will for Marlene and her child to die in that train crash?" she blurted out, no longer willing, or able, to conceal her real sense of betrayal.

Flem stared back at her, looking horrified.

"Oh, pray for me, Flem!" she cried, throwing herself into his arms. "I can't! Not now! First Floxy, then Marlene and her child and now…now my folks and Aldur are abandoning me."

Flem lifted her chin. "They're not abandoning you, min smukke. They'll be back."

"Not soon enough!" she wailed, crying uncontrollably.

"Soon enough for what?" he asked.

"I'm pregnant."

ജ്ഞ

Julie tiptoed past her brother who was fast asleep on the couch. It was a good thing that she wasn't scheduled to work today. She'd slept fitfully. Her dreams had her searching for Asher through smoldering cinders. Groggily she scooped four heaping tablespoons of England's best black tea into her teapot, just enough for her usual two cups, then two more for Roger. The poor dear had insisted on spending the night so she wouldn't be alone.

Waiting for her kettle to boil, she sat down at her bistro table and shut her eyes. Imagining herself entering the Lord's sanctuary, as Asher had taught her, she began to intercede, not only for Asher, but for all who'd been injured in the raid. A few minutes later as her kettle began to sing, Roger rushed into the kitchen waving the newspaper he'd brought with him the night before.

"Guess what? Truman has given his support to the Jewish Agency's proposal! Here," he said, thrusting it at her. "Read it yourself. Or better yet, read it aloud and I'll steep the tea. I'd like to hear it again."

Reluctantly Julie found the article and complied. "'According to a cable that Press Secretary Charles G. Ross sent to Prime Minister Attlee, President Truman has expressed support for the establishment of a viable Jewish state within Palestine. The U.S. President urged the British Mandate government to increase Jewish immigration to 100,000 immediately, then expressed his deep regret that the Palestine Conference held in London had adjourned. Truman has vowed not to support Britain's current Federalization Plan. "Only a viable Jewish state," Truman said, "will garner the support of his administration or that of the American people."'"

Julie folded the paper and laid it on the table. "I just don't understand why we haven't heard anything yet."

Roger turned around. "I didn't want to tell you last night," he said, speaking very slowly. Julie didn't like what she saw in his eyes.

"Tell me what?" she demanded. When only silence was his answer, she shook her head. "No." Roger reached for her hand, but she snatched it away then ran into her bedroom and locked the door.

ഌ

Flem slipped out of bed, not wanting to wake Liesel, and went down to the kitchen. With her hormonal changes and yesterday's trauma, she needed rest. He opened the back door. Mrs. Sorensen's lights were on, so he picked up the receiver and dialed her number.

"How did you and Caleb manage last night?"

"He's a prince, that one is. We had ourselves a delightful time."

"Well, I'm glad to hear it. We certainly didn't."

"What's wrong?" she asked.

"Our sister-in-law, Marlene, died in that train crash. Needless to say, Liesel hardly slept last night, so I was wondering if—"

"Of course, Caleb can stay, as long as you need him to. And give Liesel my condolences."

"Thanks, Mrs. Sorensen. I'll leave her a note to let her know just in case she's not up by the time I leave for Shul."

"Well, enjoy your service, and you better pray for wisdom. You're going to need it."

"I am? Why?"

"Your young man wants to know if his kitty, Floxy, is in heaven."

ഇഈ

"Is Liesel not feeling well?" Flem's father asked as they exited the synagogue. "She usually comes with you."

Flem frowned. "She had trouble falling asleep last night after everything that happened."

"Well, I'm not surprised."

"I'm afraid losing Marlene and her child has shaken her faith."

Sol stopped walking. "I'm so sorry to hear it, but heartbreak can do that. Believe me, I know. But don't worry, Son. Liesel is a strong young woman. She'll get past this. You just need to give her some time."

"Well, there's more to it than that…she's with child."

Sol gasped. "That's wonderful! Mazel tov to both of you!"

"Thanks, but I'm not finished. She also accused me of keeping secrets."

"Keeping secrets?" he repeated, making a face. "What secrets?"

"She demanded I tell her what Jacob asked me to pray about."

"He wants you in Palestine, doesn't he?"

Flem nodded. "He thinks the Lord wants me there. He's been having dreams about us, about me. He said I was smuggling Jews into Palestine."

"Ah! So that's what I've been reading between the lines."

"Making matters worse," Flem said, "Liesel, because of her hormones, I'm sure, sees her folks' move to Cyprus as abandonment, especially since Aldur is going with them."

"What about you, Flem? Will you be going to Palestine?"

Flem shrugged. "If the Lord wants me there, of course. But He'll have to make a way. After all, I have a family to support, and now a new baby on the way."

"Baby? What baby?" his mother asked, walking up behind them.

Flem turned around. "Liesel's pregnant."

Inger's eyes widened. "That's wonderful! Now I'll have two cousins I can spoil."

"Another child is exactly what this family needs," his mother said, pinching Flem's cheek. "Right, Sol?"

His father nodded. "Children are a blessing from Adonai."

"Then let's go home and celebrate," his mother suggested. "Will you join us for lunch, Flem?"

"Another time, Mother. I need to get back and check on Liesel."

"Why don't you two ladies go on ahead?" his father said. "I need a word with Flem, in private if you don't mind."

"Come on, Aunt Nettie!" Inger took her aunt's arm. "We can share secrets, too."

His father waited, watching until the women were out of earshot. "You need to ask Adonai for a sign."

"A sign? What do you mean?"

"Whatever Adonai wants is good. We both know that. What can sometimes get tricky is knowing that we've heard Him correctly. You must ask Him for a sign."

"Hmm," Flem mused, warming to the idea as snow began falling again. "What an excellent suggestion. I'll do it. Thanks, Father."

Ten

Jacob's skull felt like a scrambled egg. But his stomach was finally on the mend, well enough to have consumed most of what the hospital called breakfast. It was a far cry from Devorah's fare but when a fellow hadn't eaten in a couple of days, even creamed fish on dry toast held a modicum of appeal.

As Jacob drained the last dregs of his coffee, two orderlies wheeled in a gurney. The patient on it looked like a mummy. His inflamed face and left hand were the only parts of his body not wrapped in gauze.

"Was he in a fire?" Jacob asked.

"One of your villages got raided last night," the nurse overseeing the patient's transfer told him. "They thought this one here was a goner till someone heard him moan."

"What's his name?" Jacob asked her.

"Who knows? … any identification he might have had on him burned up with his clothes."

"If your God were merciful," one of the orderlies said, "he would've let this one die."

"Well, he'll be dead soon enough," the nurse replied glumly, "and out of his misery."

Grieved, Jacob shut his eyes. When they left, he began to pray aloud. "As a man acquainted with sorrows, take this one's pain away, Yeshua, in your mercy."

Then a raspy voice whispered, "Yeshua, hu Adon."

ꕥ

Liesel and Caleb were finishing their scrambled eggs when Flem came home. He leaned over and kissed her cheek. "How did you sleep, min smukke?"

"After we made up, quite soundly, thank you."

"Made up? Were we fighting?" he asked.

"Well, I was…but for both of us."

Amused, he sat down next to her at the table. "Which one of us won?"

"We both did. But now you have some unfinished business to take care of. Our son would like an answer."

"You promised to tell me about Floxy."

"I did, didn't I?" Flem said, trying to think of a way out of it.

It's not good to break promises," the child said then turned to his mother. "Is it, min smukke?"

"What did you just call me?" she asked laughing.

"Father calls you that."

"Well, yes, but…"

"Aren't you my beauty, too?" the child asked.

"Of course, I am, Caleb," Liesel assured him. "And you're right about not breaking promises. Only sometimes, we have to postpone them, and last night was one of those times."

"How much have you told him about what happened?" Flem asked.

"Nothing. I was waiting for you."

Flem sighed. "If you two are finished eating, why don't we go into the parlor? It'll be cozier in there."

"It will be," Liesel assured him. "I started a fire in the grate as soon as I came down this morning."

"Then what are we waiting for?" Flem asked. Shivering, he chose the wingback closest to the fireplace and had Caleb sit on his lap. "Death, Caleb, is like sleep."

The boy stared up at him looking perplexed. "But Floxy's not in bed. You put him in the ground."

"Yes, Caleb. I buried him."

"So how will Floxy get out when he wakes up?"

Flem sighed. This wasn't going to be easy, but he had to do it, had to prepare the child for the tragic news about his Aunt Marlene. "Well, when the Messiah returns all of those who love him will wake up. They'll be resurrected."

"Res…ur…rected? What's that, Father?"

"The dead will come out of their graves in new glorified bodies…bodies that'll never get sick again or die."

"But Floxy's a cat. Will cats get them, too?"

Flem sighed.

"Well," Liesel prompted, looking tickled at his predicament.

"No, Caleb. Only people—God's people—get resurrected."

The child's eyes filled with tears.

"But wolves will live peacefully with lambs, and little calves play with lions in the Kingdom."

"But I don't love lions! I love Floxy!"

"Well, since the Bible tells us about all these other animals, I'm sure cats will be there, too. You can pray about it. With God, all things are possible."

Caleb pondered that a moment. "Where's Yeshua's Kingdom, Father?"

"In Heaven," Liesel said. "That's where God's people go when they die."

Flem cocked his head. "The restored Kingdom will be on Mount Zion, Caleb, in Jerusalem, where Adonai placed His name."

"Then will Floxy go to Jerusalem in his old cat body when he wakes up?" Caleb asked.

Liesel jumped out of her chair.

"What's wrong?" Flem asked.

She ran out of the room without answering.

"Is Mother crying because Floxy won't get a new body?"

"No," Flem said, realizing what he'd done. "I said something that upset her."

"Did you lie?"

Flem set Caleb on his feet. "No, Son, but I was thoughtless. Now, I want you to stay here and play with your toys while I go and apologize."

Caleb grabbed Flem's pantleg. "Wait, Father!"

"What?"

"Will you apologize to min smukke for me, too?"

"For you? Why?"

Caleb shrugged. "Because I love her."

ꕤ

Jacob forced himself out of his hospital bed then waited to catch his breath. When he felt steady enough, he crossed to the far side of the room and positioned himself behind one of the chairs that were lined up in front of the window. Using it as a walker, he pushed it toward the bandaged man's cot. Then the ward's double doors opened and a nurse, one Jacob hadn't seen before, spotted him and turned red.

"Just what do you think you're doing? You know you're not allowed to get out of bed unassisted. Do you want to fall and get another concussion?" she asked, prying his fingers off the back of the chair.

"I need to be able to hear what that man's saying."

"What man?"

Jacob pointed to the bed next to his.

The nurse rolled her eyes. "I'll tell you what he's saying. Nothing. Not a word. Can't you see he's all but dead?"

"He spoke to me, I tell you, and in Hebrew at that! I heard him."

"Then, you're delusional!"

"I'm not dead," a low, muffled voice said. "Not yet."

Color drained from the nurse's ruddy cheeks. She turned and dashed out of the ward.

Jacob pushed his chair toward the man's bed as fast as his legs would take him. "What's your name?"

"Zelenko…Asher Zelenko. I heard your prayer."

Jacob smiled. "How's your pain now?"

"Better," he said as the ward's doors flew open.

A doctor, with three nurses trailing him closely, rushed over to Asher's side, then the doctor locked eyes with Jacob. "Get that one back to bed where he belongs."

As two nurses flanked him, the third nurse yanked on the privacy curtain cutting off Jacob's view.

Eleven

Flem searched the kitchen, their bedroom, and Liesel's sewing room to no avail. Then he dialed Mrs. Sorensen. Heavy hearted that the widow hadn't seen Liesel since she picked up Caleb earlier, Flem went back upstairs and checked each room again. He was about to go back down when what sounded like scraping stopped him. It seemed to be coming from Caleb's bedroom. Rushing into it, he spotted the attic ladder. It was pulled onto the floor.

"Liesel, I'm sorry. Please come down." He waited but she didn't respond. "I want to apologize, min smukke."

"I don't want to talk to you! Go away!"

"I wasn't thinking. You have to believe me."

"Fine! I believe you. Now will you go away?"

"If you don't come down here, I'm coming up."

Flem lifted his foot but as he was about to step on the bottom rung the ladder began moving. He jerked it back down and started up.

"You have nothing to say that I want to hear," Liesel said as Flem's head cleared the opening. She was sitting cross-legged on the floor in front of Katlev's old cedar chest. Flem shoved the old man's books aside to make room for himself.

"You really scared me. I looked everywhere but here. I even called Mrs. Sorensen."

"Great! Now she knows we're fighting."

"All she knows is that I was looking for you…and that I love you very much." Flem reached for Liesel's hands.

She snatched them back. "What you love is to torment me!"

"That's not true!" Flem said.

"Then why do you do it?"

"Remember how you used to quote the New Testament trying to convince me that Jesus was the Messiah?"

"I remember that you refused to accept it as Scripture."

"Do you?" Flem asked.

"Do I what?"

"Accept the New Testament as Scripture."

"Every word!"

"Including what Yeshua told some Pharisees?"

"Be specific. I'm not sure what you're getting at."

"He told them they loved their traditions more than they loved God's Word."

Liesel's face turned red as she scrambled to her feet. "Tradition or not, heaven is a lot more comforting than…"

"More comforting than what, Liesel? The resurrection?"

"More comforting than Marlene rotting in a grave!"

"But, min smukke, the dead know nothing Scripture says. When Marlene resurrects it will seem like mere seconds."

Liesel swiped at her tears. "Not for me, it won't!"

Flem pulled her into his arms. "Go on, cry. It's healthy to grieve, only not like those without hope." He took out his handkerchief and gently dried her face, and this time, his wife didn't resist him.

ഌഎ

"What's the weather doing out there?" his father asked as Aldur entered the sitting room.

"It looks like one of Marlene's snow globes turned upside down."

His mother, who was sitting next to his father on the sofa, looked up from her crocheting. "It's a good thing you stayed here last night. If this wind keeps up, we might lose our power, and your flat doesn't have a fireplace."

"We wanted to save money," Aldur told her, pacing in front of the window.

"I'm not criticizing, but I do wish you'd sit down. You're wearing out the carpet."

Aldur shut the drape. "It's this weather. It's making me claustrophobic."

"Then pour yourself some schnapps and relax," his father said.

"I don't want any. I need a clear head."

"To do what?" his mother asked.

"To write a letter of resignation and plan my wife's funeral."

His parents exchanged looks.

"Your mother and I have discussed this, and we want to cover the costs of Marlene's interment."

"I appreciate that, Dad, but she's my responsibility."

"Then pay us back over time," his mother told him. "You need to save your money for Cyprus…unless, of course, you prefer living with us."

Aldur smiled at her cunning. "I'll think about it, Mother."

"While you're thinking about it," his father said, "you might want to consider telling us why you suddenly hate your job."

"I will, Dad, once we're in Cyprus."

ℵℑ

Matityahu hated hospitals, especially those in Palestine, so he nudged Devorah a little closer to the information desk. When she turned and frowned, he knew she got the message.

"Excuse me," she said to the attendant. "Can you tell me what room Jacob Mitzger is in?"

The matronly female laid down her magazine and glanced over at her open log. "He's in the second ward. It's right down the hall on your left. But you can't go back to see him for another five minutes. Visiting hours haven't started yet. Have a seat over there." She pointed.

"What about last night's raid?" Matityahu asked. "Can you tell us how many were killed?"

"We're a hospital, my good man, not a morgue."

Matityahu struggled to hold his tongue or at least keep it civil. "Then can you tell us how many were injured?"

"Sorry. That information is privileged."

"All my husband wants to know is how bad it was."

"You'll find all those answers in this morning's *Palestine Post*." She pointed again. "It's on that table over there."

Matityahu rolled his eyes.

"I'll get it, Mati. Go and sit." Devorah lowered her voice. "And remember your blood pressure."

"Where's the paper?" he asked when she returned a minute later empty-handed.

"You don't want to read it now, Mati dear." She sat down.

"I most certainly do!"

"No, you don't. It's still Shabbos and we're here to cheer Jacob up not depress him."

Knowing that meant the headlines weren't good, Matityahu sighed heavily, watching the minute hand on the wall clock move slowly to the right. When it at last reached the twelve, he stood up. "Let's go," he told Devorah.

"How's that poor head of yours?" she asked Jacob, holding his hand over the bedrail.

"It feels like a scrambled egg."

Matityahu smiled. "Then be glad your name's not Humpty Dumpty."

"You look and sound so much better than the last time I saw you," Devorah told him.

"I can walk now, too! Only, my wardens here won't allow it."

"They will once you're stronger," she assured him then turned. "Mati dear, will you bring us some chairs?"

"So, tell me," Jacob said. "What do you think of Nurse Abercrombie? Isn't Julie a delight?"

"She's lovely," Devorah told him as she sat down.

"Those puzzles in the newspaper, the ones with all the little dots, what are they called?" Jacob asked.

"Connect-the-dots," Matityahu informed him.

"Yes, yes, that's it! And Yeshua, I've discovered, is the Great Dot Connector!"

Matityahu leaned over and felt Jacob's brow. "No. You've not got a fever, but you might need to stay here a little longer, my friend."

"Behave yourself, Mati, and sit down," Devorah scolded. "I think I know where Jacob's taking his little analogy."

Matityahu rolled his eyes. "Then perhaps you should be admitted as well."

"See the fellow in the bed over there?" Jacob pointed. "Do you know who he is? He's a disciple of Yeshua's … and the man is a sabra."

"What happened to him?" Matityahu asked, horrified at his blistered face.

"He's a survivor, one of the few, from last night's raid."

Devorah gasped. "Really? What's his name?"

"Zelenko," Jacob said. "Asher Zelenko."

Twelve

By the time the Havdalah candles separating the Sabbath from the rest of the week were lit, the wind had spent most of its fury and Flem's stomach was growling. He tiptoed up behind his wife in the kitchen and slipped his arms around her waist.

"Can I help with anything?"

"Dinner will be served in twenty minutes, but since you asked," Liesel said, turning to face him, "would you mind going back up to the attic? I forgot to put Katlev's books back in the chest."

"My pleasure, min smukke." He kissed her cheek. "I'm going to pray after that so just call me when we're ready to eat."

ꕥ

Devorah was so excited, the minute they got home she dialed Julie's number.

"She must already know that Asher is there," Mati told her, opening the fridge. "After all, she works at the hospital, doesn't she?"

After several rings, Devorah hung up. "She's not answering her phone."

"Try Roger?"

"I would, but I don't have his number."

"Ah, but I do," Mati told her as he took out the leftover rugelach. "You'll find it in the top, left-hand drawer of my desk."

Devorah patted his cheek. "Mati dear, you're the best!" With her other hand, she snatched the pastry away.

"What are you doing?" he demanded.

"I love you, Mati dear, and don't want you should spoil your supper."

As she replaced their leftover dessert in the Frigidaire, Mati rolled his eyes. "Well, you have a strange way of showing it, woman!"

From her husband's office, Devorah dialed Julie's brother. "Shalom, Roger. This is Devorah Goldberg. I'm trying to reach Julie, but she's not answering her phone. I was hoping you might be able to—"

"Hope no more. Julie is right here with me."

"Well, you and she need not worry if you've read this morning's edition of the *Palestine Post.* What they reported wasn't quite true."

"What do you mean not true?" Roger asked.

"There was one more survivor in last night's raid," Devorah told him excitedly, "not just the three women."

"Stop beating around the bush, Devorah. Tell us what you know!"

"Asher is alive! He's in the hospital, in a bed next to Jacob's."

"Are you certain that it's Asher?"

"He's in serious condition, Roger. But Jacob prayed for him, and his pain is now much improved. But Asher is badly burned … he's wrapped up like a mummy."

After a long pause, Devorah heard Roger whisper, "Asher is alive" at the other end of the line. Then she heard Julie gasp.

"He's in the hospital…in Jacob's ward," Roger explained before returning to their conversation. "Thank you ever so much for phoning us, Devorah, but I must hang up now. We'll be in touch with you soon."

"Well, visiting hours are over, if you're planning to go see him."

"Not for my sister they aren't. Wild horses won't keep her away!"

ഌ

Flem donned his tallit in Liesel's sewing room, which doubled as his prayer closet, and got right to the point. "Adonai, there's no need for me to elaborate on everything that's happened since You already know the situation better than I do. As for my going to Palestine, if You want me there, I'm more than willing, You know that. But You'll have to make a way. I've got a family to support with another child on the way, and Liesel already feels like she's being abandoned," he said as Liesel knocked on the door.

"Stew's ready. Come on down."

"I'll be there in a minute," he told her, then waited to hear her footsteps recede. "Please comfort my wife. She's taking Marlene's death really hard, and being pregnant…Well, You know what's she's going through."

ഌ

Liesel stifled a yawn, crawled under the covers, then moved over to make room for Flem, who stooped and kissed her lightly on her forehead. "Sweet dreams, min smukke."

"You're not coming to bed?"

"I will in a little while. I want to pray some more first. You don't mind, do you?" he asked, wondering what he would say if she told him that she did.

But Liesel didn't. "Go on," she told him, stifling another yawn.

Flem blew her a kiss, then left the bedroom.

Before retrieving his kippah and tallit from the drawer he stored them in, he spotted Katlev's book and picked it up. The title, *Christian Jews*, had caught his attention when he went back up to the attic at Liesel's request to put the rest of Katlev's collection back in the cedar chest.

Intrigued by its title, he opened the musty volume to the first chapter then sunk into his overstuffed prayer-chair and began to read about a Jew named Gregory Abu'l Faraj Bar-Hebraeus, who was born in Melitena, Greece in 1226 C.E. There he was evangelized by his father, a respected Jewish physician, who came to believe in Yeshua in his youth. When Gregory turned twenty, he moved to Antioch, where he studied theology. He became proficient in Hebrew, Greek, Syriac, and the Arabic language. Flem was impressed until he read that this Messianic Jew later converted to Catholicism and became the Bishop of Gubus.

Flem turned to the second chapter about a Jew named Solomon Halevi, who was born in Spain in 1351. Hoping it would leave a better taste in his mouth, he continued to read. But Halevi, the Rabbi of Burgos who wrote an exegetical commentary on Isaiah 34 that garnered him wide acclaim, eventually converted too, after meeting several times with Christian theologians to discuss Thomas Aquinas' writings… and researching all the Old Testament's Messianic prophecies. In 1390, Solomon and his entire family converted. Then this former rabbi went on to earn a doctorate in theology from the University of Paris.

Mystified, Flem shut the book.

Yeshua's apostles never stopped being Jews… neither did Paul. Now the author did say that Halevi continued to midrash with Jewish scholars and even wrote a play about Purim but that still didn't explain why he did what he did.

Too tired now to pray, Flem got up. Tomorrow, after shoveling snow, he would go visit his father. Hopefully, he might shed some light on why these Jews who knew their Jewish Messiah felt it necessary to relinquish their God-given identity.

ꝏ

"He won't be awake now. I just gave him a hefty dose of morphine not ten minutes ago."

"But I only want to see him," Julie begged, praying.

The charge nurse frowned. "Then go, if you must."

"You're an angel," Julie said over her shoulder, running down the corridor.

"This is highly irregular," the nurse continued, "and I intend to say so in my report."

Three patients lay sleeping in the second ward, but only one of them was wrapped in gauze from his head to his feet.

Asher's swollen face brought tears to Julie's eyes. She'd been a nurse long enough to know that a patient could survive second-degree burns on seventy percent of their body, but not third-degree burns on over fifty percent of their flesh. Even with massive doses of penicillin, such a patient would become septic. Neither surgical debridement nor applying hypochlorite solution would be enough to save Asher's life. Only a miracle.

ꟾ

By late morning, Flem's fingers, even in his fleece-lined gloves, felt numb from shoveling snow. In the kitchen he pulled them off then ran hot water over his hands, hoping to thaw them.

Liesel handed him a towel. "Ready for some lunch?"

"I'm really not hungry."

She glanced up at the clock. "Well, would you mind watching Caleb for a while? I'd like to drive over to my folks and check on Aldur."

Flem placed the hand towel on the counter. "I've got a better idea. Why don't I drop you off? Then I'll take Caleb with me to visit my parents."

"Perfect!" Liesel said. "I'd rather not drive on these streets anyway."

"What time do you want me to pick you up?"

"In a couple of hours, I guess, unless Aldur wants me to go with him to his apartment so he can pack a few things. I'll phone your parents and let you know."

ꟾ

When no one answered, Flem hoisted Caleb onto his hip. He was about to let himself in when his cousin Inger flung the door open. "I need to speak to my father. Do you know where he is?"

"No, but Aunt Nettie's in the kitchen."

Flem set Caleb down on his feet. "Would you mind watching him for a while?"

"Mind? Of course not," she said.

"I'm her prince," Caleb said, glancing up at his father. "Aren't I, Cousin Inger?"

Flem smiled and ruffled the boy's hair.

"Thanks," he told Inger and headed into the kitchen where his mother had her hands submerged in dishwater.

When Flem sneaked up on her from behind and hugged her, she gasped and spun around. "You nearly scared me to death, Flem!"

"Scared you? I thought for a moment you were about to slug me."

"And you would've deserved it if I had," she told him, laughing.

"Is Father up in his library?"

"He's in the tub, soaking away all his aches and pains. He's been shoveling snow."

Flem smiled. "Well, I know just how he feels."

"Did Caleb come with you?"

"He's with Inger," Flem said, turning to leave.

"Where are you going?" she asked.

"To check on Father."

"I told you he's bathing."

"Well, he might need his back scrubbed," Flem said, not divulging his real purpose.

When he reached the bathroom, he tapped lightly on the door then let himself in. "You're taking a bubble bath?"

"And what if I am?" his father demanded.

"You look like Father Christmas," Flem told him, amused by the foam on his father's beard.

"If you're through making jokes, would you mind shutting that door? You're letting in a draft…and this happens to be foaming

Epson salts not bubble bath. What are you doing here, anyway? Why aren't you home taking care of your pregnant and grieving wife?"

"Liesel's visiting Aldur at her folks."

"How's she holding up?"

Flem shrugged. "It's been rough. I found her up in the attic yesterday with Katlev's books."

"Liesel was reading Katlev's books?"

"She was hiding from me."

"Hiding? Why?"

"She was upset by something I said, but it's okay. We made up."

"Well, I'm glad. This is no time for the two of you to be arguing about anything. Your pregnant wife needs your support."

"Have you ever heard of a man named Gregory Abu'l Faraj Bar-Hebraeus or a Messianic Rabbi named Solomon Halevi?"

"No, can't say that I have. Why?"

"He lived in the fourteenth century."

His father arched a foam-covered eyebrow. "There were no Messianic rabbis in the fourteenth century, Flem."

"He wasn't one for long…a rabbi, I mean. He converted to Catholicism and later became an Archbishop. I read about him in one of Katlev's books, one titled *Christian Jews*, that should have been titled, *Conversos*, if you ask me. I found it most disappointing."

His father sighed. "I guess the world wasn't ready for us then, Flem. As Jews they would've been outcasts from both worlds."

"Katlev knew the truth. So does Jacob and Matityahu, and both are still rabbis. There must be others like us, Jews who know their Messiah, Yeshua."

"Hand me that towel, would you? I'm starting to feel like a prune."

"There's a Scripture," Flem said, passing him the towel, "in Acts, I think. It mentions a myriad of Jews coming to faith in Yeshua who were all jealous for the Torah."

His father stood and wrapped the towel around his waist. "Do you remember when I called you 'my dear deluded son?' "

"Remember? I'll never forget. You said there'd be no Jews left if

Hitler and the Mufti had their way."

"What I said was idolatrous, Son!"

"Idolatrous? What do you mean?"

"I had more faith in what the British Mandate government declared than I did in God's Word. You must never make that mistake, Flem!"

Flem smiled. "That's for sure. Katlev made me promise something very similar once."

"Did you?"

"Did I what?"

"Make the promise," his father said.

"I did!"

"Good! Now tell me, what have you heard from the Lord?"

Flem sighed. "Nothing yet, I'm afraid. I'm still waiting."

ꕥ

When Jacob awoke the next morning, he spotted a woman curled up in the chair next to Asher's bed. A moment later, when a crashing sound from the adjoining ward startled her, she sat upright in her chair.

"Good morning, Nurse Abercrombie!" Jacob said.

"Boker tov, Jacob, and please, call me Julie."

"How long have you been here?" he asked her.

"Since last night…and thanks for praying for Asher's pain. Devorah told Roger it really helped."

"Well, Asher certainly helped mine."

"You should start feeling like your old self again in a week or so."

"That's not the pain I meant," Jacob said, smiling.

"Is it your stomach, then?"

"It was my heart," Jacob said, causing Julie to look alarmed.

"I thought the Goldbergs and I were the only Jews in Palestine who knew our Messiah."

Julie visibly relaxed. "Well, there are at least twenty that Asher and I know personally… and probably many more. One fellow he told me about escaped from Dachau, which was a miracle in itself. Then he parachuted into Palestine with the help of some Danish pilot in the underground," Julie told him as she cranked up the head of his bed.

Then Asher began to groan and she rushed over to him.

ꕥ

Mordi Ginzburg glared at his typewriter, disgusted with himself and unable to focus. At twenty-four, he was already the youngest editor-in-chief of not one but two publications—the *Hillel News* and the *Mercury*, a glossy humor magazine. And every month, Mordi pounded out a book review for the *Commentary*. And, if that weren't enough, in three more months, he would become an ordained rabbi.

So why did he feel like such a loser? He was doing what he'd been born to do. Write! Except, every sentence now seemed so trivial, and it was when compared to what he knew in his heart, if not his head, would soon take place across the Atlantic. History would be made.

The fulfillment of prophecies that Adonai gave to Mordi's people thousands of years before would soon become manifest. Yet here he was sitting behind his desk in New York, nothing but a prosperous and worthless putz, a Jew about to become a rabbi, who had broken the vow he'd made to his congregation on the day of his Bar Mitzvah back in 1935.

"To be a faithful Jew to God and our people, I must be faithful to the Land," he'd told those assembled. "I must learn about its past—its prophets, its seers, and scholars. It isn't merely the Land of our patriarchs, it's our future, our redemption, the end of our exile! After centuries, our people are returning to their inheritance, building up Israel, and making the desert bloom.

"But sadly, at thirteen, I can't help them," he'd said. "But I vow before you and God that I will in days to come! Our values have taken root in my soul. Our concepts of a nation stir in my heart and will never be erased. As I step over the threshold into manhood today, I promise that once I am legally of age, I will make Israel my home. For as Yehuda Halevi once wrote, 'Bedam va'esh Yehuda nafla. Bedam va'esh Yehuda takum! Fortunate is the man who lives in your streets, to see the good of your chosen, and to rejoice in your happiness as you (Israel) return to the days of your youth.'"

Tears filled his eyes as he recalled the way his voice cracked, how emotion forced him to pause before delivering his closing remark. "With blood and with fire, Judea fell. We lost our homeland. Now, with blood and with fire, it's time for us to take our Land back!"

All these years later, Mordi was now more certain than ever that it was no coincidence that he had made Alyiah, a return to the Land, within seven days of his bar mitzvah. The world referred to it as Palestine, but it was still the Holy Land. The land God granted to Mordi's people in an irrevocable covenant, and that land included all of the territory those Red Coats who were now in charge renamed Trans-Jordan and ceded to Jew-hating Arabs.

The year he spent there with his family was the best in his life. In the Land, Mordi learned to dance the Hora. During Chanukah, with hundreds of other students, he paraded through Tel Aviv's winding streets carrying hanukkiahs and flaming torches. Tel Aviv was exciting, but Jerusalem captured his heart. With his passion to write, he had volunteered to help with his school's Hebrew magazine, which in turn helped him master the Hebrew language.

Halfway through their stay, he became enamored with the Hagenah. In every Jewish settlement, young Jews, many his own age, gathered three times a week to learn how to shoot. Those modern-day Maccabees practiced with rifles, pistols, and with whatever firearm they could lay their hands on.

Mordi knew what he had to do. He'd finish his book review for the *Commentary* and mail it in with his resignation. On Monday, he would phone the *Mercury* and terminate his position, then go down in person and disenroll from seminary. For now, he would hang onto his position as editor. It would make it easier to get on with the *Palestine Post* if he already had a job. Then he would apply for a student visa, for he knew, sadly, that immigrating there would take years.

Thirteen

On Monday, December 23, as soon as Flem entered the *Gazette*, Geørg waved him into his office. "Shut the door and sit down. We need to talk."

"Is there a problem?" Flem asked as he took a seat.

Geørg snatched a page off his desk and waved it around. "I'm disappointed in you, Lund."

"What did I do?"

"It's what you didn't do that concerns me. You've written some terrific copy for me in the past, so I know you've got it in you, Lund. I also know that you've been wanting to cover harder news for some time now."

"I do!"

"Then explain this!" he said, waving the page again.

"Did I write something I shouldn't have?"

"Oh, no. That would've been too easy for me to fix."

"Then I don't understand."

"There's no heart in this, Lund! Not in one single sentence of your miserly paragraph."

Flem slumped in his chair knowing that Geørg was right.

"You'll have to do better if you're serious about keeping Müller's beat."

"May I ask you a question?" Flem humbly asked.

"What?"

"Well, if it was that bad, why did you print it?"

Geørg's face turned crimson. "What choice did you leave me? You dropped it on my desk and left. We have deadlines around here! Remember?"

Flem shut his eyes. "I promise you it won't happen again. There were some extenuating circumstances."

"Save your excuses. I don't want to hear them!"

"Sorry," Flem said.

"Now, against my better judgement, I'm going to let you slide this time. But I warn you, Lund! I won't again. Next time you'll be out of here. Understood?"

"Yes."

"Good! Now go! I've got a paper to run."

Flem stood as Glinda, Geørg's secretary, entered the office and smiled at him solicitously. "Good morning, Flem. Please give my condolences to your family. It must've been awful for you, having to identify your sister-in-law's body in all that wreckage."

Flem nodded. "It was…"

"When is her funeral?" Glinda asked. "I'd like to go."

"Tomorrow at eleven," Flem said.

"Well, I'll be there…that is," she turned to smile at Geørg, "if the boss will give me the time off."

Geørg hung his head between his hands and groaned.

Glinda shrugged, then dropped Geørg's mail on his desk and left his office.

"Are we finished?" Flem asked him.

"Not yet!"

"I already gave Jim Yung all the particulars for Marlene's obit."

"I wish you would've given them to me."

"To you?" Flem said, confused.

"Then I wouldn't have made such a fool of myself."

Understanding, Flem smiled. "It's okay, Geørg, no hard feelings. Are we done?"

"Not quite. I have something you need to take home and read." He opened his drawer then handed Flem an envelope.

"What is it?" he asked.

"It's your new job description. Just be sure that you read all the fine print before signing it."

ᘓᘐ

Flem opened the front door, too excited to hang up his overcoat. Liesel wasn't in the kitchen. He checked the dining room and found her setting the table with their very best china.

"Are we expecting guests tonight?" he asked.

She glanced up at him, smiling. "No, just celebrating."

"Ah! So Geørg phoned you with the good news. He felt pretty bad about chewing me out the way he did."

"Chewing you out? What're you talking about?"

"Geørg didn't call you?" Flem said, confused as Caleb tugged at his overcoat.

"We're celebrating me, Father!"

Flem picked his son up. "And just what is it about you that we're celebrating, young man?"

The boy held up some fingers. "I'm … I'm almost four now and … and I don't spill things … not like I used too. Right, min smukke?" he asked, turning to his mother.

Liesel smiled. "No, dear. You don't."

"Now I can eat in here with the grownups."

"That's wonderful, Caleb." Flem ruffled the boy's tresses. "I'm proud of you, Son."

"So why did Geørg chew you out?" Liesel asked.

Flem set Caleb down then reached into his pocket. "Müller's job is now officially mine," he said, waving his job description. "Or it will be once I sign my new contract."

"That's wonderful, Flem. I know how much you've been wanting this."

"Well, you want it, too, don't you?" He scooped her into his arms.

"It will mean more money, and we have a new mouth to feed."

"Whatever makes you happy, dear. Now go take off your coat so we can eat. Then I want you to tell me everything, why Geørg chewed you out."

As Flem cryptically related Geørg's tirade to keep Caleb from hearing too much, since they'd still not told him about Marlene's accident, Liesel stood up.

"Well, I'm glad that Geørg finally did the right thing," she said starting to clear the table.

Flem slid his chair back then stood up. "Me too. Now it's time for bed, young man."

"Why can't I stay up with you and min smukke?"

"Because you need your rest," Flem said.

"But I'm almost four!"

"Your father needs to put you to bed now so he can go up and pray," his mother told him in her no-nonsense tone.

"I can help you with the dishes first," Flem offered.

"I want an answer from the Lord, Flem. Now get out of here, both of you."

ᘓᘐ

Eager to thank Adonai, for Scripture declared that promotion comes from the Lord, Flem laid his job description on the table next to his prayer-chair then grabbed his tallit and kippah.

Forgoing the traditional blessing for donning a prayer shawl, he shut his eyes. Then blinding light filled the sewing room. Flem fell to his knees.

"Because your heart and walk please Me, I will demonstrate My power to you and through you, once again. In the fullness of time, I will turn your defeat into victory. So do not despise small beginnings."

With the fading of the light, Flem's heart began to pound. "What about Jacob's dreams? Where do you want me, Lord?"

"Read your job description," came the whisper.

ꕥ

Liesel yawned, hoping Flem would come to bed as soon as she changed into her night clothes. She poured four-fingers-worth of sherry into a goblet for Flem and set it on the nightstand next to her juice. He entered the bedroom looking dazed as she recorked the wine. "Are you okay?"

"I just had a vision…or a visitation. I'm not sure which it was, but the Lord spoke to me, Liesel. He spoke to me audibly."

"He did what?"

Flem collapsed next to her on the bed. "Light filled the room."

"Are you serious?" she asked, handing him his sherry.

"I wouldn't make up something like that!"

She stared at him speechless.

"He told me that I pleased Him."

Liesel remained silent.

"You don't believe me, do you?"

"I believe that you believe it," Liesel said.

"Then you don't believe me!" he said and stood up.

She grabbed hold of his hand and pulled him back down. "I know the Lord speaks to you, Flem. But you've told me yourself, and on more than one occasion, that He does it through Scripture."

"Yes, and sometimes the Lord speaks, and this time He used audible words."

"What did He say?" Liesel asked, trying not to sound doubtful.

"That He would demonstrate His power both to me and through me and that, in the fullness of time, He'd turn my defeats into victory."

"But what does that mean, Flem?"

"He also told me not to despise small beginnings."

"Aren't those all quotes from the Bible?"

"So? What if they are?" he asked.

"You've been praying for an answer to give Jacob."

"I asked Him that too."

"Well, what did He say?"

Flem hesitated. "He told me to read my job description."

"Your job description?" Liesel could no longer hide her incredulity. When the phone started ringing, she bit her tongue to keep from saying what she was thinking and picked up the receiver.

"Sorry to be calling you this late, Mrs. Lund, but may I speak to your husband? This is Geørg Drøhse."

"Certainly!" Liesel held out the phone.

"Who is it?" Flem asked.

"Your boss."

"What does he want?"

"Ask him yourself!" she told him.

Flem took the phone. "Hello, Geørg…Really?...Yes, I did, just a little while ago. Why?...Oh, I see." For several minutes, Flem just listened. His expression began to change. "Yes! Of course, I will!"

"What's he saying?" Liesel asked.

"I really appreciate that, Geørg…Absolutely! You can count on it," Flem said then hung up.

"What did Geørg want?"

Flem drew in a long breath. "He's sending me to Palestine."

"Palestine? You can't go! Marlene's funeral is tomorrow."

"I won't be flying out until Thursday evening."

"When will you come back?"

When Flem hesitated, Liesel knew he was about to tell her something she didn't want to hear.

"For three months."

Her eyes filled with tears.

Flem pulled her into his arms. "It's the Lord's plan. I didn't understand it myself, not really, until Geørg called, but I do now."

Not mollified, she pulled away from him. "Well, bully, bully for you! Because I don't!"

"There's a clause in my contract about 'times of unrest' during which the *Gazette* can send me out of the country for extended periods."

"But three months?"

"It'll likely be longer, Liesel, but I'll get two weeks' vacation every three months. So, I'll be back to see you."

"To see me?" Liesel covered her face.

"Geørg wants me splitting my time between Palestine and Cyprus, so I can visit your folks and Aldur, too."

Liesel stopped her crying and lifted her head. "Did you say he's sending you to Cyprus?"

"It's bad timing, I know, with you being pregnant and all."

"Please, Flem! I need to think!"

She jumped up and began to pace. After circling the room twice, she sat back down on the bed and picked up the receiver.

"Who are you calling?"

"My parents."

"At this hour?"

"I have to let them know that Caleb and I will be going with them."

ꙮ

Tuesday, December 27th, 1946
Baltimore, Maryland

The wind chilled John Bark to the bone. But at least it had stopped snowing. Determined not to allow winter to dampen his spirits, John climbed into the back of the cab with Steven Greenbaum and Bill Bernstein. A mile down the road, when the streets grew narrower and the neighborhood became a slum, John began to pray.

When they reached Pier 8 on Lancaster Street, the first thing John noticed was the pier's rotting timbers beneath patches of melting snow.

Greenbaum climbed out next. "That's the *Warfield?*" He turned to John. "Do they really expect us to run British blockades on that piece of crap?"

Lost for words, John simply shrugged.

Next to him Bernstein sniffed the air. "What's that awful smell?"

"There's a chemical plant down the block," the cabbie explained as Bernstein crinkled his nose.

"Well, it smells more like garbage."

"Oh, that," the cabbie said. "That's runoff from the sewage. Now which one of you is paying my fare?"

John handed him two one-dollar bills and said, "Keep the change."

Smiling, the taxi driver got out and opened the trunk. Then he set their bags on the sidewalk.

Greenbaum stared at him. "This is nuts! You know that don't you?"

John shrugged, attempting a smile. "The Lord split the Red Sea, didn't He?"

Bernstein groaned. "Well, if we're really going to do this, let's do it now before I lose my nerve."

"I know she doesn't look like much," John said, grabbing his bags, "but according to Captain Ash, the ship's hull is in excellent shape."

Bernstein rolled his eyes. "You're beginning to sound like a used car salesman, Reverend."

"All I know," Greenbaum said, "is we've got a lot of hard work ahead of us."

"But it's doable!" John said as they made their way onto the ship. "And we won't be working alone."

"Easy for you to say, I can't even drive a nail in straight."

Bernstein playfully punched Greenbaum's arm. "You rich kids are all alike."

"What's that supposed to mean?" Greenbaum asked.

"When it comes to doing anything practical, you're worthless."

John was about to add his own two cents when a guy who looked like a teenager came up to them and extended his arm.

"You must be that Methodist preacher we've all been hearing about. I'm Bernie Markus, the first mate, and the only one aboard, so far, with sea legs."

The firmness of the kid's grip impressed John.

"We were beginning to wonder if you guys were ducking out on us," Bernie continued as three other crew members joined them.

After introductions were made, Bernie told them to grab their bags. "I'll show you where you're bunking. In a few hours when the rest of our crew is aboard, we'll eat."

Curious, John asked, "Where'd you grow your sea legs, Bernie?"

"Merchant Marines. I came up through the ranks. I now hold membership in the Masters, the Mates, and the Pilot's Union."

"If you don't mind my asking," John said, hoping his question wouldn't offend their first mate, "how old are you?"

Bernie grinned. "I know I don't look it—or so everybody tells me—but I'm twenty-four."

Bernstein whistled. "Well, blow the man down!"

When Bernie flushed a deep crimson, John knew he was going to not only like this curly-haired sailor boy but respect the lad, too.

"A few other seasoned sailors will be joining us," Bernie quickly pointed out, to take the attention off himself. John liked that, too. "One of them graduated from the Merchant Marines Academy at Kings Point."

"Well, that's great," Greenbaum said. "Because we sure aren't seamen. Although, I did take a couple of sailing lessons when I was a kid."

"Really? Why'd you give it up?" Bernie asked.

"The boom whacked me in the back of the head," Steven said, then everyone laughed.

"Well don't let that discourage you," Bernie told him. "Most of our volunteers don't know squat about ships either but with Ash as our captain, I assure you, by the time we reach Marseille, all of you will! That is, if you can survive the captain's tongue-lashings."

"Who are the others that'll be joining us?" John asked. "What are their backgrounds?"

"We're a mixed bag," Bernie told him. "Some ex-G.I.'s, Marines, sailors, several clerks, and college students with nothing to offer except enthusiasm."

John smiled. "The Lord certainly had a sense of humor when He put us together. We'll be a regular Gideon's Army. Correction, a regular Gideon's Navy!"

"Technically," Bernie said, "since we'll be doing our job on land and water, we'll be Gideon's Marines."

꧁꧂

Before her afternoon shift on Tuesday, Julie felt Asher's brow. "You're burning up! I'll get the nurse."

"You're my nurse, Julie. Please don't go!"

"But I'm not the one with a key to the medication cabinet."

"Morphine won't help. It'll only put me to sleep, and I need to say goodbye."

Tears filled Julie's eyes. "No, you're not leaving me! I won't let you!"

"We'll see each other when Yeshua returns."

"But I don't want to say goodbye. Not yet! I'm not ready! Do something, Lord!" she cried.

"He has, my love. Now you must do something, Julie."

"Anything, Asher. Just ask."

"Run your race and don't hold back! You have much still to accomplish. I've already finished mine, and done it well," he said, his voice growing weaker, "thanks to you, my love."

Then his eyes closed for the last time.

꧁꧂

On Thursday afternoon, December 26th, Flem removed his tallit and his kippah. To say that he was amazed at how the Lord had worked out everything would've been an understatement. His precious, pregnant wife would now be cared for in the bosom of her family and Aldur would have his sister's companionship to see him through his bereavement.

"My folks are here," Liesel called up to him from downstairs.

Flem went out to the banister. "I'll be down as soon as I get the trunk shut."

Less than a minute later, his father-in-law stood in the doorway. "I thought women were the ones who over-pack."

"A woman did!" Flem told him.

"My daughter did that?"

Flem shrugged. "She's the only woman in my life except my mother, and she never got the chance."

"Think we should both sit on it?" Dr. Prestur asked.

Five minutes later, they'd lugged the old steamer chest down the stairs and set it next to the front door.

"Give me a minute to catch my breath," Flem said, "then we can take it out to your car."

"Didn't Liesel tell you? The plan has changed."

"Aldur is taking you," Liesel explained. "And I'm going along for the ride."

"Whose staying with Caleb?" Flem asked.

"He'll spend the night with us," Liesel's mother told him.

"Aldur will be staying here tonight. Sorry, I forgot to tell you," Liesel apologized as a knock sounded at the door.

When Liesel opened it, Aldur looked chilled to the bone. "Sorry I'm late. I stopped by Marlene's grave to change out her flowers. But don't worry." He glanced at his watch. "We've got plenty of time to get you on the plane."

"Why?" Flem asked. "You know they'll be frozen in an hour."

Aldur shrugged. "I passed the florist this afternoon and her favorite roses were on display."

Hearing it, Flem's heart broke.

"We understand," Liesel said, stroking her brother's arm. "Don't we, Flem?"

"Of course," he agreed, a bit embarrassed.

"Well, I better run up and check on Caleb. Our son is packing what he'll need for tonight," Liesel said, then whispered in Flem's ear. "My folks have offered to explain what happened to Marlene."

"Praise God," Flem said, relieved.

Dr. Prestur held out his palm to his son. "Give me your keys, Aldur. Flem and I can get his trunk into your car. You look half frozen. Why don't you go warm up in front of the fire."

Mrs. Prestur linked arms with Aldur. "I'll join you. We can chat a while."

Ten minutes later, Flem was ready to go. But as they went out to Aldur's automobile, he kept feeling like he was forgetting something.

"Sit in the back with your wife. I'll play chauffeur," Aldur told him.

"Great minds think alike," Flem said, making doe eyes at Liesel as he slid next to her. "I'll get over to see you as soon as I can, min smukke. I promise."

"I wish you didn't have to leave this soon with the New Year so close," she said, snuggling next to him.

"Me too, min smukke. But I'll be thinking about you, both of you, as I ring the year in.

"Well, just don't celebrate too much or you might forget!"

"Forget?" Flem said, disturbed by the word.

"What's wrong, Flem. You looked worried."

"I keep getting this nagging feeling that I've forgotten to do something important."

"Do you have your visa?" she asked.

Flem patted the pocket of his overcoat. "I do."

"You got that thing awfully fast," Aldur said, watching them through the rearview mirror. "Transit visas usually take weeks, and sometimes even longer."

"Geørg pulled some strings," Flem explained. "And he usually gets what he wants."

Aldur nodded as he pulled away from the curb. "Give Jacob and the Goldbergs my best. Tell them I'll get over there for a visit when I can."

Flem smacked his forehead. "That's it!"

"What is?" Liesel asked.

Flem turned to look at her. "I never phoned Jacob to let him know that I'm coming."

Fourteen

As soon as Flem disembarked the plane, two agents from the JAI, the Jewish Agency for Israel, headed toward him, dodging several taxi cabs that were pulling into the terminal. Ten minutes later, after they questioned him at length about his purpose for being there, the senior agent handed Flem a business card. "Please feel free to contact us if you think we can help you with any problems."

"Any problems?" Flem repeated, not clear as to what the agent meant since the JAI helped Jews immigrating to Palestine and he was there on behalf of the *Gazette*.

Then it dawned on him. The JAI also worked, covertly of course, with the Hagenah to smuggle Jews who'd been turned away due to the government's restrictive immigration quotas.

"I'll be sure to do that," he told them, remembering Jacob's dreams, "should I run into any."

"Then we understand each other?" the senior agent asked.

"We do," Flem assured them.

Smiling, they tipped their hats and walked away.

Excited about what the Lord might have planned for him, Flem hurried into the terminal.

An hour and a half later, after finally making it through customs and exchanging his money for Palestine pounds only two cabs remained. Just then, an Arab rushed into the back of one of them. When it pulled away from the curb a moment later, Flem approached the only taxi left. "I need to go to West Jerusalem."

"Too late go there," the Arab driver said. "Can take to nice hotel in Tel Aviv."

"I don't want a hotel in Tel Aviv. My boss has already made arrangements for me to stay in West Jerusalem."

"No hotel West Jerusalem."

"I'm not checking into a hotel. I'm renting an apartment that belongs to a friend of his."

"Tomorrow rent house. Tonight I take to nice hotel."

Struggling to not lose his patience, Flem spoke slowly. "I do not want to go to a hotel! I want to go to West Jerusalem!"

"My wife, she want Fahid to go home!"

"Why are you being so difficult? It's only an hour drive and I promise you that I'll be more than generous with your tip."

"Not one hour," the driver said, "one hour fifteen-minutes. Be two-hour, one half by time Fahid get back."

"Fine! I'll double your fare then!"

When the cabbie narrowed his eyes, Flem knew the man was considering it.

"For triple, Fahid take. Get in!"

"For triple," Flem told him, no longer attempting to remain calm, "you'll help me get my luggage into your trunk!"

When the cabbie's eyes widened, Flem feared he might drive off and strand him there. He was about to apologize when the Arab suddenly smiled.

"Where West Jerusalem I take?"

"Rehavia," Flem said, silently thanking the Lord.

"Boss' friend must be wealthy man."

"What makes you think that?" Flem asked as the driver got out of his taxi.

Fahid rubbed his thumb in a circular motion against his fingers. "Need money! Plenty money live there."

ꙮ

Early Friday morning Matityahu awakened suddenly. Knowing that he'd never fall back to sleep and that Devorah was a light sleeper, he sat up slowly on the edge of the bed and allowed his feet to find his slippers.

"Where are you going, Mati? It's not time to get up."

"I need to pray," he told her.

"You can pray in the morning!"

"It is morning," he said, snatching his robe off the chair.

Devorah rolled over. She grabbed the alarm clock. "It's four o'clock, Mati! We went to bed five hours ago. If you don't get back in bed, you'll be grumbling all day."

"The Lord can refresh me," he retorted clutching his tallit.

"Well, then peek in on Jacob before you start. I don't like the way he looked last night. He seemed foggy."

"The poor man is recovering from a concussion. What do you expect? But I'll check on him, so go back to bed or you'll be so contentious I'll have to hide from you on the roof."

When his wife's pillow struck his jaw, Matityahu smiled and shut the door behind him. Quickly, he crossed the walkway to Jacob's bungalow. Not wanting to disturb him, he didn't turn on the light but only listened. Hearing no breathing, Matityahus grew anxious. He flipped on the wall switch.

"Jacob, are you okay?"

No response came.

Matityahu walked over to the bed. Then his stomach turned to stone. His friend's lips were blue and his chest wasn't rising. Tears blurred Matityahu's vison as he prayed for wisdom…the wisdom to find the right words to break the news to Devorah that Jacob had passed.

ꕥ

In spite of the barbed wire perimeters and the soldiers patrolling on nearly every street, the ancient city of Jerusalem was nothing short of beautiful. He'd been walking its limestone paths for nearly an hour, unable to decide exactly where he would enjoy his first breakfast in the Land. His bungalow, though stocked with every accoutrement he could possibly imagine or need, Flem knew it would never compare to a meal eaten with the sabras in the old city. But where? There were so many to choose from.

Flem checked his wristwatch.

Liesel had promised to phone the Goldbergs at 9:00 a.m. to let them know he'd arrived. It was only 8:15 now. He toyed with hailing a taxi and just surprising them. But that would be inconsiderate, so he surrendered to the aroma wafting from a small café across the way.

ꕥ

Matityahu felt numb but he had to remain strong, or at least pretend, for his wife's sake.

"It's all my fault!" she wailed. "I should've phoned Julie last night when he didn't look right."

Matityahu took hold of her hands. "Stop beating yourself up and get dressed."

"But Julie could've had him readmitted to the hospital."

"To do what? Die there instead? Go on and cry. It'll make you feel better," he said, handing her his handkerchief. Then the telephone began ringing.

"Would you mind answering that, Mati? I can't talk to anyone…not now."

He picked up the receiver. "Shalom. Who is it?"

"I have a person-to-person call for Rabbi Jacob Mitzger. Can you put him on please?"

"I'm afraid he's no longer with us."

"Do you have a forwarding number for him?"

"Jacob passed away last night. Who's trying to reach him?"

At the other end of the line, Matityahu heard a gasp. Then a woman's voice said to the operator, "Let me speak to him instead."

"I'll bill your call station-to-station then," the operator replied before clicking off.

"This is Liesel, Fleming Lund's wife. Am I speaking to Rabbi Goldberg?"

"You are." He motioned Devorah to come closer so she could listen.

"My husband will be devastated. He flew into Tel Aviv late last night."

"Flem is here? Where is he staying?"

"In Rehavia, West Jerusalem. He was hoping to spend this Sabbath with all of you, but I'm sure he'll understand."

Devorah snatched the receiver out of her husband's hand. "This is Devorah, and we would love nothing better than to have Flem spend Shabbat with us! His presence at our table will make it a lot easier to bear our loss…and he can sit shiva with us for Jacob."

"What's shiva?" Liesel asked.

"It's the traditional seven-day mourning period," Matityahu explained.

"Well, Jacob certainly made our grief over losing Katlev easier to bear. In a strange way, Jacob became Katlev for us. The night he showed up on our doorstep, he told us that Katlev had bequeathed us to him."

When Matityahu blinked away tears, Devorah handed him back his handkerchief.

"Now Mati and I bequeath ourselves to both of you," Devorah said. "I know Jacob would have wanted that."

"Make sure you tell my husband. He's going to need family over there."

"How long will he be here?" Matityahu asked.

"At least three months…possibly longer."

"I take it this isn't a pleasure trip then," Matityahu said.

"He's now the *Gazette*'s foreign correspondent. I almost said war correspondent, but let's pray it doesn't come to that. Every three months he'll get two weeks' vacation but will be there until things settle down."

"That must be a challenge for you and your son," Matityahu told her.

"Not really. He'll be splitting his time between Palestine and Cyprus. My father has accepted a position at a D.P. Hospital over there, and Caleb and I will be going with them."

"Then you must come visit us," Devorah told her excitedly.

"I would love that," Liesel said. "But I really must hang up now. I'll be thinking of you, all of you, when I light the Sabbath candles tonight."

Devorah glanced at her husband. "And we'll think of you and little Caleb!"

"Shalom," Matityahu told her. "Have a blessed New Year!"

Devorah hung up the receiver. "Mati, this is truly a blessing! God has sent us the one and only person who could truly share our grief. It's the best possible medicine, don't you think?" she asked her husband as a knock rattled their door.

ꕥ

Julie choked back tears. "But he looked so much better the last time we spoke!"

Roger shrugged. "Matityahu informed me that they took his body away two hours ago. His funeral's the day after tomorrow since tomorrow is the Sabbath."

"Why didn't they call me?" Julie asked.

"They tried, your phone kept ringing busy."

Julie sighed. "I had to take it off the hook last night because some drunk kept calling here looking for Florence," she said, putting the kettle on, "and I forgot to replace it when I finally got up."

Roger frowned. "Have you been sleeping any better?"

"Sleep? How can I sleep? I'm only tired when I'm at work."

"Have you prayed about it?" Roger asked.

Julie turned away, pretending to adjust the flame under the burner so she wouldn't have to look at him. "I can't pray, Roger! Not now!"

Grasping her shoulders, Roger forced her to face him. "Why not?"

"I want to know why. Why, Roger, with all the vile people in this evil world, did God find it necessary to take a kind, gentle, loving man like Asher?"

Roger pulled her into his arms, but she was in no mood to be comforted. She pushed him away.

"I know you don't want to hear this right now, Julie, but the Lord is the only one with the answers you're looking for."

"Well, I don't want His answers! I want Asher back! And Jacob, too!" she said, swiping at her tears.

"Don't hold it in, Julie. Go ahead, have a good cry, a good long one."

"I don't have time!"

"Of course, you do."

"Not if I don't want to be late for my shift," she said as the kettle began whistling.

Roger shut off the burner. "Then call in…tell them you're sick. You need to rest."

"I can't! Not if I'm taking Sunday off for Jacob's funeral."

"Then request leave. Or better yet, take a vacation. You haven't had one in some time."

Julie stared back at him in silence. Should she tell him now or wait to hear from her commanding officer?

"What is it, Julie? What aren't you telling me?"

She took a deep breath knowing there was no time like the present. "I requested a transfer to another duty station."

Roger stared back in disbelief. "After all we went through to get stationed here together, you want to leave?"

"I have to, Roger. I can't stay here after everything that's happened. Every time I walk into the second ward, I see Asher…his face. I have to get away! But you've no need to worry. If my transfer comes through, and I don't know that it will since I've not been here a year, I won't be far away. We can still see each other often."

Julie reached for her brother's hands, and he squeezed them.

"Where will you be going?"

"To a hospital in Cyprus for Displaced Persons. They're in dire need of nurses."

ഌଓ

Flem knocked at the Goldbergs' door, but there was no answer. He checked his watch. Surely Liesel would've called them by now. He was about to sit down on the steps and wait, when a woman's voice from inside said, "I'm coming…I'm coming."

A moment later, the door opened.

"Mrs. Goldberg?" Flem said, tentatively in case it wasn't her.

"You must be Fleming Lund. Come in! Come in!"

"Did my wife phone you?"

"She did, and please call me Devorah. Mati will be with us in a moment. He's changing his clothes right now."

"Mati?" Flem said, not recognizing that name.

"Matityahu, my husband," she explained, leading Flem into another room. "I'm the only one he allows to call him that… although Julie got away with it once or twice."

"Who's Julie?" Flem asked as a man, who could only be Rabbi Goldberg, rushed into the parlor and offered Flem his hand.

"What a great blessing this is, to finally meet you, Fleming."

"I'm blessed to finally meet you, both of you," he said, smiling at Devorah, "and I can't wait to have a good long visit with Jacob again. Is he here?"

The couple exchanged looks, then Devorah motioned him to one of her armchairs. "Make yourself comfortable while I go and brew us some tea."

Flem complied, but her husband remained standing after his wife left the room.

"There is no easy way to tell you this, Fleming. But Jacob passed away last night."

For several seconds Flem could not speak.

"He died in his sleep. His mission here was accomplished."

"What does that mean?" Flem asked.

"Every life when it's submitted to Elohim serves a purpose, Fleming. Jacob could not have breathed his last breath had Adonai more for him to do."

"I never thought of it that way before," Flem said, still finding it difficult to form words.

"You look like you could use some fortification," the rabbi said, crossing over to the sideboard, "or is it too early for you to imbibe?"

"Normally it would be. But please go ahead, Rabbi. I need it."

"I haven't been called rabbi for many years now, Fleming. I'm just a farmer these days, so please call me Matityahu."

"Would it be alright if I just call you Mati? I'm Fleming but everyone calls me Flem."

Mati smiled. "I warned Devorah this would happen. First Julie, now you. I suppose Roger will be next. So why not?" he asked, pouring a second glass. He handed it to Flem. "I hope you like Moscato. It's Devorah's favorite."

Mati sat down.

Flem took a sip. "It's quite good. Thank you … do they know what caused it? Was Jacob sick?"

"He was recovering from a concussion."

"He fell?"

"You might say that," Mati said as Devorah returned.

"Here I've been fixing tea for us and you two are guzzling wine, and it's not even noon yet."

Flem smiled. "Mati was just telling me about Jacob's fall."

"Jacob's fall? Jacob didn't fall! He was stoned outside of Jaffa Gate."

"I was about to explain how it happened," Mati said defensively.

"Then please, by all means, continue," Devorah told him. "I'll just sit here and listen," she said, taking the chair next to Flem's, "just in case you leave something out."

Matityahu frowned. "When they took Jacob to the hospital, a most incredible thing happened. His nurse was—"

"Mati, Mati, you must first explain why Jacob was there and what he was doing!"

"I have a better idea," Mati said as his wife's kettle began screaming. "Why don't you tell him, since I'm making such a poor job of it?"

Fifteen

On the Sabbath, December 28th, winter rains pelted Jerusalem, but the sun shone on those gathered for Jacob's funeral the next day. After the interment, Flem rode back to the Goldbergs' in a cab with Roger Abercrombie and his sister, Julie. Conversation at the Goldbergs' dinner table was subdued. For Julie, Flem noticed, it was almost nonexistent.

Mati rose from the table when the ladies got up to clear away the dishes. "Excuse me, but I must go and feed my chickens."

As he left the room, Flem turned to Roger. "Is your sister okay?"

He shook his head to the negative. "The night we came to let the Goldbergs know that Jacob was in the hospital, Asher, the sabra who drove us, got called away by the Hagenah. Arabs were raiding a village not far from here, and this time they used explosives."

"Was he killed?" Flem asked.

"He survived but not for long. He had third degree burns over most of his body. As a nurse, Julie knew that only a miracle could save him, but Asher didn't get one…and he was a believer."

"In Yeshua?"

Roger nodded. "He died Tuesday and was buried on Thursday."

"Julie was in love with him?"

"Madly. And now she's mad at God."

ꙮꙮ

On December 30th, a bomb exploded on the third floor of a bank building in Haifa, killing two Jews and injuring five early that morning. It was Monday and Flem's first day on the job. So after only three hours of sitting shiva for Jacob at the Goldbergs', he called for a taxi to take him to Haifa to investigate the bombing. The next day, in reprisal for doing little to nothing to stop the Arab attack, the Irgun Underground blew up the British Officer's Club.

The morning after New Year's Day, which was anything but festive in Jerusalem, Flem typed up the tragic event:

On Tuesday, December 31st, fifteen members of the Irgun underground blew up the British Officers Club housed in the Goldschmidt House on King George Street in Jerusalem. A janitor at the Alliance Girl's School, which was closed for a teachers conference, confessed to leaving the gate open for the Irgun. Once inside, the underground changed into confiscated British Army uniforms in one of the empty classrooms, then left in a taxi. A van filled with the Irgun fighters followed their cab to King George Street. But finding several British Army trucks parked in front of the Goldschmidt House, the Irgun circled the block several times. Once the British trucks left, Yitzhak Avinoam, the Irgun's District Commander, gave the order to begin their mission.

The first unit positioned itself across the street from the Officers Club, next to the Yeshurun synagogue, and aimed their Bren gun at the building that housed British soldiers in case they interfered with the Irgun's operation. The second unit, positioned on King George Street in front of the Goldschmidt house, fired several rounds in the air to stop traffic so another van could crash through the barbed wire fence. When two guards who were patrolling the house approached the van and demanded to see their entry permit, the Irgun opened fire, providing cover to other members of their group, dressed up like sappers, who ran into the building with thirty kilograms of explosive. After igniting the fuses, they escaped through a hole in the fence between the synagogue and monastery that had been cut earlier in the day.

Irgun girls met them there with satchels of clothes they could change into. Once emptied, the sacks were used to conceal the Irgun's weapons and British uniforms. At exactly 3:30 p.m., the Goldschmidt House exploded, killing eighteen British officers and wounding twelve.

Flem stared at his copy, knowing he couldn't submit it to Geørg, not without revealing his source, and he couldn't. He wouldn't. It felt wrong somehow. Even the strange way his informant appeared out of nowhere then disappeared felt almost mystical.

Flem yanked the page out of his typewriter and stood up. Then he walked into his kitchenette and burned it on the stove. After clearing away the ashes, he sat back down in front of his typewriter and began to type again:

Three weeks ago, the *Lanegev*, a two-masted ship flying an Italian flag set sail in Sète, France with a cargo of emaciated Jewish refugees the Aliyah Beit had hoped to smuggle into Palestine. But the vessel, built in 1875, was no match for the British destroyer, the H.M.S. *Chieftain*.

Off the coast of Haifa, in the wee hours of the morning yesterday, the H.M.S. *Chieftain* blocked the *Lanegev*. The crew and passengers fiercely resisted, but in the end, the British Navy boarded the vessel. One elderly displaced person was transported to a hospital in Palestine where he later died. The rest of the Jewish refugees—395 men, 181 women, and 60 children—were forced to board the H.M.S. *Empire Heywood* and were deported to Cypress.

Satisfied with this one, Flem checked his watch. He had just enough time to wire his article in Nahlaot then take a cab out to the Goldbergs'.

ꕥ

At one in the afternoon on Sunday, February 16th, the crew of the future *Exodus* assembled on the main deck where the *Warfield*'s passengers once dined in elegance. Every Zionist in Baltimore was there. They wanted to be able to tell their children and grandchildren about a crew of mostly young American Jews and a Methodist man of the cloth who were about to swear an oath.

I faithfully swear to the Hagenah Ha'ivri of Eretz Yisrael to uphold its constitution all the days of my life. Unreservedly, I take upon myself a call to serve at any time and place, to obey its commands, and to faithfully fulfill its instructions, and, if necessary, to sacrifice my life for the redemption of Zion.

After their swearing in, each member was presented with a sweater bearing the Hagenah's insignia and a Hebrew Bible, everyone except John who was given a Christian prayer book and the bottle of champagne that would christen the ship the *Exodus* when they reached France.

Then the master of ceremony introduced Captain Ash, the man who made their mission possible.

"We've all had to abide the captain's temper and tongue, but without his expertise none of us would be standing here."

The gathering grew quiet.

Then one man stood up and started clapping…then another, and another. Soon everyone was applauding.

Looking humbled, probably for the first time in his life, John mused, Captain Ash cleared his throat. "I know I've never told you how proud I am of what you're doing, but I should have. You're twentieth-century Maccabees. Only, this time, instead of fighting the Greek Army," Ash said as his voice began to crack, "you'll be taking on the British Navy."

The cheers that remark elicited continued for several minutes.

Then John was up next. But after Ash's heart-felt comments everything he'd planned to say seemed somehow trivial. John decided it would be best to simply tell them what was on his heart.

"I'm sure you're all wondering what a Christian clergyman is doing aboard a ship that's about to smuggle over four thousand Jews into Palestine."

Laughter rippled through the crowd.

"I can best explain it by telling you of an event that occurred in

Italy near the end of the war. Close to sunset one Friday, several Jewish soldiers, bivouacked next to a Catholic monastery, decided to hold an Erev Shabbat service. But they needed a minion and only had nine. Then one of them, spotting a statue in the monastery garden, got an idea. 'Hold on,' he told them, jumping up. 'I'll be right back. I found us another Jew.'" John paused, fighting back tears. "It's because of that Jew, whose Hebrew name means salvation, that I have sworn, if necessary, to sacrifice my life for the redemption of Zion."

ཀཀ

February 17

Disgusted by the British High Court's decision to reject the Jewish community's habeas corpus plea that would have saved eight hundred Jews from being deported to Cyprus, Flem folded his *Palestine Post.* He just didn't understand how the Court, after acknowledging that the H.M.S. *Ocean Vigor* detained those poor refugees under horrid conditions on the high seas, could uphold the High Commissioner's unsubstantiated claim that all eight hundred of them presented a threat to the peace in Jerusalem, in spite of the fact that the high-handed magistrate admitted under oath that he had not checked a single Jew's record.

Flem set his empty mug in the sink, then checked his watch. It was time to get going. In twenty minutes, the strike called for by the Yishuv to protest the High Court's decision would begin.

ཀཀ

With his sister's help, Aldur finished boxing up all the little, and the not so little, mementos he wanted to keep, things like the camera he gave Marlene a week before she died. When she had teased him that he really bought it for himself, he had denied it, of course, but the next day he had bought her the emerald ring she'd been wanting, the ring she was wearing when he buried her nine days later.

"Are you sure you want to sell all of your furniture?" Liesel asked.

"I need the cash to rent a place of my own."

"I thought you were staying with our folks?"

"Not for long."

"Does Mother know?"

"I've mentioned it to her in passing. Have you seen the telephone directory anywhere?"

"It's on the counter in the kitchen. Why?"

"I need a number for an auction house."

When the phone began to ring, Aldur snatched up the receiver. "Yes? What is it?"

"Is that how we taught you to answer the telephone?"

Aldur grinned. "This is the Prestur residence. May I help you?"

"Packing must not be going well," his father said. "Hopefully, my news will improve your mood."

"What news?" Aldur asked.

"You have a hospital position waiting for you in Cyprus, if you want it."

"But I'm not medically trained."

"You can drive, can't you?"

"What am I driving?" Aldur asked glancing over at his sister.

"An ambulance, of course! It's a hospital."

ઙઌ

Julie stared at the document in her hand. Her transfer had come through so quickly she wasn't sure if she was happy about it.

"Well," her supervisor said, frowning, "I expected you to look pleased."

"Oh, I am," Julie lied, "just surprised."

"I certainly hope so. Because there is no turning back now. Your position here has been filled. You're to report to the hospital in Cyprus in seven days. Any questions?"

ꙮ

After helping to take on the last of their provisions in the wee hours of the morning, John Bark made his way to the bow of the ship. Transfixed by the holiness of the occasion, he thanked the Lord again as the *Warfield* pulled away from the pier. When they entered the first swells of the Atlantic, he returned to his cabin to document the event.

He'd just opened his journal when a determined wave sent the volume of poetry that he always kept on the nightstand reeling across the cubicle. When it collided with his boot, John picked it up.

Lord Byron's *Hebrew Melodies* had belonged to his wife, Laura.

In college, on their very first date, John listened, enthralled, as Laura informed him of all the anti-Semitic reviews the book received. The *British Review* labeled Byron the poet laureate of the synagogue. Another warned that "young lords are never better off for meddling with Jews." A few, however, like *Gentleman's Magazine*, called Byron's verses elegant.

Since Laura's death, *Hebrew Melodies* had become John's most treasured possession. Her notations allowed him to hear the lilt in her voice again. He opened it to "Weep For These" and read it for the hundredth time. It was Laura's favorite. The last verse he read out loud.

"The wild dove has her nest, the fox his cave, Mankind their Country—Israel the grave."

In the lower left corner, Laura had penned Jeremiah 31:10 Hear the word of the Lord, you nations! Proclaim it in distant coastlands! He Who scattered Israel will regather and watch over His flock like a Shepherd.

ꙮ

That night the waves rocked John to sleep, but just as they cleared the Capes in the morning the weather grew fierce. By noon, the wind velocity had reached sixty miles an hour. The ship began to struggle.

All but seven of the *Warfield*'s forty-two crew members were heaving their guts out over the rails.

"We might have to turn back," Captain Ash told his first mate. "They're stumbling around like a bunch of drunks."

"I put the sickest ones in cabins on the hurricane deck in case we have to abandon ship."

"We can't abandon ship!" John said, appalled at the very thought of it.

Captain Ash scowled. "I never said we were abandoning ship! But if the storm doesn't let up soon, we're heading back to the Chesapeake."

"I'm going back to my cabin and pray," John told him.

"Of course, you are!" the captain retorted. "That's about all you're good for, isn't it?"

John stopped. He was about to turn around. Then he decided to let it go, to count it all joy, like the Apostle Paul said to do. Besides, Ash's question was obviously a rhetorical one.

ꕥ

Seventy-five miles east of the lighthouse in Diamond Sholes, known as the Graveyard of the Atlantic, Captain Ash left the bridge to check out the engine room. What he found wasn't good. The ship was in danger of flooding. If that happened, the tub would lose power immediately.

Ash pulled out his handkerchief and mopped his brow. He hoped Bark actually had influence with the Almighty because they were going to need it. Then he dropped to his knees, a position he'd not assumed in decades, and bowed his head.

ꕥ

At 9:00 p.m., the U.S. Coast Guard and two other ships in the vicinity escorted the *Warfield* to safe harbor. John Bark pulled on his rubber boots as Captain Ash and Bernie—along with less experienced sailors like Bernstein, Greenbaum, and himself—got ready to dive into the brig in rubber coveralls—that Steven Greenbaum had dubbed Jesus suits—to salvage as many provisions as possible.

That the doors had remained watertight and that the pump handled the flooded areas was nothing short of a miracle. The old barge was still afloat with her superstructure intact, but only just barely.

At 4:00 p.m., the following afternoon, the *Warfield* anchored in a quarantine section in Hampton Roads. There, several crewmembers were put ashore for medical treatment. The next day, the *Warfield* docked at a rickety old pier halfway between Norfolk and the Navy Base.

Captain Ash addressed the crew, fit to be tied. "Why didn't you idiots seal up the chain pipes? Whattaya think we store ready-mix cement for? And why in God's name did you drive her so hard? What kind of seamen are you? Don't you know you're supposed to slow down when the sea's up? You nearly sunk the ship and now we have to replace $23,000 worth of supplies. Why, if it were up to me, I'd sack every last one of you!"

Sixteen

Several weeks later, in preparation for the *Warfield* to be moved to another shipyard where all her major repairs could be made, the chief engineer put the engines in reverse. But when he did, the throttle went over too far, causing the pistons to thrash and the propeller to bite deep. The *Warfield* surged forward then backwards, then she shot astern and charged into the channel taking with her several of the pier's rotten pilings. It was then, while watching their latest catastrophe, that Captain Ash began wondering if all those rumors he'd heard about the old *Warfield* being jinxed might be more than just legend.

Once the *Warfield* finally docked at the Brambleton Shipbuilding & Drydocking Company later that rainy afternoon, most of the crew went ashore to enjoy the bright lights of Norfolk.

Ash turned to one of the few men who remained, hoping he wouldn't choke on his words when he asked the good reverend to pray. "We need money for all these extra expenses, John. Our situation is dire."

"Why not hold a fundraiser?"

"We can't do that!" Ash told him then quickly moderated his tone. "The British might get wind of what we're up to and then, pardon the expression, our ship will be sunk."

"They won't find out if you're careful," John said, seeming not to have taken offense. "Contact your cadre of donors by word of mouth only."

Ash pondered the reverend's suggestion, but not for long. What choice did he have? He needed to raise the cash and fast if they were to continue their endeavor. "Would you be willing to head up the drive?"

John beamed. "Be glad to, Captain! But I'll be needing all the names of your big money men and their phone numbers."

Ash clasped the reverend's arm. "Then let's go back to my cabin."

ຮOଔ

Three weeks later, after every repair had been made to the captain's satisfaction—and paid for—Ash called a meeting to introduce the new crew members he'd hired to replace the five land-lovers who bailed on him after that storm as well as his new chief engineer. After the introductions were made, Ash opened the meeting for questions.

"How much longer are we going to be here, Captain?" Greenbaum asked.

"One more week and we'll be on our way. We have commitments to meet in the Mediterranean, and the Hagenah is getting antsy because of all these delays."

"Do you think she'll make it across the Atlantic this time?" Bernstein asked with a smirk.

It caused Ash to bristle. "Of course, she'll make it! The *Exodus* is seaworthy in every way!" he replied but much too brusquely. When several of his original crewmembers began to murmur, Ash knew he had a problem. He also knew that it wasn't as much about the seaworthiness of the *Exodus* as it was about him. Rightly or wrongly, a few of his crewmembers were still sore at him for the tongue-lashing he gave them after the storm. Ash was about to do the unthinkable and ask their forgiveness when Steven Greenbaum jumped out of his chair.

"Listen up, you guys. We're gonna make it! We're gonna sail this old crate all the way to France, pick up our refugees, and smuggle them into Palestine. So, knock off the bellyaching!"

ၡ৩

Flem could hardly believe it was already Sunday, March 2, 1947, when he ripped February off his desk calendar and pitched it into his waste basket. Events—mostly bad ones—had been happening so fast and on such a regular basis, he could hardly keep up with them. But conflict sold papers, so Geørg, of course, was happy.

On February 14th, the British Mandate government had petitioned the United Nations for help to solve their Jewish problem. For Flem, that request was the one and only bright moment during the entire second month that held a modicum of promise. But not all of the Jews in Jerusalem felt the same, because most of the nations represented by the U.N. were historically anti-Semitic. Not to mention the phrase "Jewish Problem" smacked of Hitler's "Final Solution."

But in spite of it all, Flem felt hopeful. As King Solomon once wrote in the book of Proverbs, "A king's heart is like a stream of water in the hand of Adonai. He directs it wherever He wants." And that, Flem knew, included the hearts of the UN delegates.

Flem checked his wristwatch. He had to get moving. The *Ocean Vigor* would be docking in Haifa in one hour with the year's quota of 1,500 legal Jewish immigrants from Cyprus.

ၡ৩

Studying the long line of somber immigrants waiting to board British buses that would disperse them to various Jewish settlements scattered around Palestine, Flem felt drawn to a bedraggled teen who flashed him an exuberant smile.

"I'm Fleming Lund," he said in Hebrew, rushing over to the lad. "I'm with the *Gazette* and would like to interview you."

The youth turned his head to one side, squinting. "No talk English?"

"Of course! I'm just surprised that you do," Flem said.

The boy smiled. "Learn in camp. Speak Romanian much better."

"And not Hebrew?"

"Speak Yiddish very well."

"Where did you live before being interned at Cyprus?"

"Romania."

Flem's heart broke. The Romanian dictator, Antonescu, had exterminated 400,000 Jews between 1941 and 1943.

"Almost killed, but Adonai make miracle. Make Yehuda not seen."

"Not seen?" Flem said. "Do you mean the Lord made you invisible?"

"Invisible, yes! Adonai's angel make Yehuda invisible!"

Heart racing, Flem opened his notepad. "What's your name?'

"Grünbaum… Yehuda Grünbaum."

Flem scribbled as fast as he could. "Go on, I'm listening."

"Fleas, many fleas, in Bogdanovka camp. Guards forced both sick and not sick in stables to be burned."

"The fleas?"

"Jews."

"Did they have Typhus?"

"Some, but not all… not Yehuda."

Flem was about to ask him another question when a British soldier raised his bullhorn. "Listen up! The busses are leaving in five minutes, so form a line in front of each one and snap to it!"

"Sorry, must go now," Yehuda said.

Thinking fast, Flem dug in his pocket for his business card and a few shekels. "Here, take this and call me as soon as you're settled. I can't wait to hear more about Adonai's angel and how he made you invisible."

In Cyprus, miles of glimmering sand and crystal-blue water proved to be just the tonic Aldur needed after such a bitter winter. Reluctantly, he rolled up his towel after laying on it for over an hour, ignoring his mother's warning. But now it was time for him to go back to the house and change. Then, he would grab his camera and explore more of the island before going to work.

ᢁᢂ

Liesel hung up the receiver as Aldur burst through the front door. "Aldur, I have great news! Unless the situation over there goes crazy, Flem's coming to spend the weekend."

"If it goes crazy?" Aldur said. "It is crazy from what I've been reading."

Ignoring her brother's cynical comment, she followed him into his bedroom. "I can't wait to tell Caleb. He's going to be so excited."

"Do you mind?" Aldur said, turning around. "I need to change."

"Use your screen! I need to talk to you."

"I don't have time. My orientation is this afternoon."

Liesel glanced up at the clock. "It's only a quarter to twelve. Your interview isn't until two."

"But I have things I want to do first."

"I'll only keep you five minutes. I promise."

"Fine!" Aldur said.

"Julie Abercrombie, the nurse whose grandfather treated Sima for that snakebite, was transferred to Father's hospital. I'm inviting her to dinner Friday night."

"That'll be nice, having a nurse as a friend, with you being pregnant and all."

Liesel frowned, then chose her next words carefully. "She could be your friend, too."

Aldur poked his head around the side of the screen. "What are you up to, Liesel? I won't have you playing matchmaker!"

"But both of you have lost someone you love … you could

comfort each other."

"I don't need comforting … I need to be left alone!"

"But the Bible says we're to comfort one another."

"Give it up, Liesel! I'm not interested!"

"But Aldur—"

"Look, if and when I decide I need a girlfriend, I'm perfectly capable of finding one myself. I don't need your help!"

"I just want the two of you to meet."

This time Aldur stepped from behind the screen. "Since you're inviting Julie to dinner on my day off, how can we not meet? But I'm warning you, Sis, no matchmaking!" Aldur grabbed his camera case. "Do I make myself clear?"

ᢀ

Aldur's heart sank when he saw the ugly tents, metal huts, and barbed-wire fencing that surrounded the detention camp. British soldiers armed with rifles monitored the perimeter from strategically placed towers. Except for a couple-dozen adults, who couldn't be a day over thirty, most of the incarcerated were twelve to eighteen-year-olds.

Aldur sighed as he checked his watch. He had two hours left so he'd snap a few photographs then head back to check out those cottages he'd passed. They were about ten minutes from the hospital and had a For Rent sign in front of the office.

ᢀ

Excited about his conversation with Yehuda, Flem decided to stick around and have lunch at the Hotel Zion before he headed back to Jerusalem. After looking over the menu, he handed it back to the waiter. "Bring me your salmon salad."

"What can I bring you to drink?"

"Water with lemon would be nice."

"That's all?"

Flem smiled. "I don't need alcohol if that's what you mean. I'm already drunk, and it's not from wine. V'lo me-yayin!"

The waiter shrugged.

As the hotel's lunchtime trio began playing Broochim Habaim—blessed are those who've come—Flem couldn't stop thinking of how many times Adonai had rendered Katlev's old cutter invisible to German patrol boats. He was certain that his brief encounter with young Yehuda wasn't a coincidence, and that it wouldn't be his last.

ജ്ഞ

The cottages were sad, if not downright shabby. But since he was already there, Aldur decided to go in and check them out.

In the office, an elderly woman sat mending a man's shirt. "Yes, please," she greeted him without bothering to look up. "What I can do for you?"

Recognizing her accent, he smiled. "Are you Greek?"

Her head jerked up. She peered at him suspiciously over her spectacles. "Of course, Greek! No Turk here!"

Aldur restrained his amusement. "I'm Aldur Prestur. I'd like to see one of your cabins."

Exerting some effort, the old girl rose from her chair. "Thalia show .... come," she said wobbling behind the desk. She snatched a key off a hook. "Follow me."

As the old woman stuck her key into the lock of the unit next to her office, her phone started ringing. "You look! Thalia answer telephone."

"Take your time," Aldur told her, preferring to check the place over by himself.

What he saw inside pleasantly surprised him. The furnished sitting room, kitchenette, and bath had freshly painted walls. There was even a back door that had to lead somewhere. The only problem he found with the place was its lack of a bedroom, and the sofa in the sitting room wasn't long enough for him to sleep on.

Then he noticed the rectangular molding on the wall with a brass handle at the top. Hoping it might be one of those pull-down hide-a-beds, he went over to check it out.

Sure enough, it was. With that problem solved, he opened the back door to a tiny, enclosed courtyard with no grass. Still, the enclosed yard held great possibilities. He would rent the bungalow today if the old gal wasn't asking too much for it.

Seventeen

Flem returned from Haifa exhilarated but exhausted. Intending to read the Scriptures for a while, he stretched out on the sofa but his eyelids kept drooping. So, he shut them instead. Hopefully, Yehuda would contact him before Friday. And if not, when he got back from Cyprus, Flem would flash his press card and schmooze a few bureaucrats to get the name of the youth's settlement.

After twenty minutes of daydreaming, Flem forced himself to get up and go into the kitchen to fix a salad. He'd just set the lettuce on the counter next to his tomatoes and mushrooms when a knock sounded at the door. Hoping it might be Yehuda, Flem hurried to find out.

"Shalom. Sorry to disturb you. I'm looking for my friend Elias Eskolski."

"He's out of the country at the moment," Flem told a sportily dressed man in his early twenties. "But he'll be back next week. Elias is my editor's old school chum, which is why I'm renting his studio. Or I should say why the *Gazette* leased it for me." Flem extended his hand. "My name is Fleming Lund."

The man shook it firmly. "I'm Mordechai Ginzburg, but everyone calls me Mordi."

"Your English sounds American."

"I'm from New York. And as of today, I'm the foreign editor of the *Palestine Post*… for the next five months, at least."

"Why only five?" Flem asked.

Mordi shrugged. "Their editor needed some time off, so we'll see what happens after that."

Flem stepped aside. "Would you like to come in? I was about to make a salad. Care to join me?"

Mordi smiled. "I'm here, so why not?"

ଛଓ

Over a salad and bagels with cream cheese, Flem grew to like the *Palestine Post*'s latest Foreign Editor—liked his wit, his preciseness in choosing words, and especially Mordi's passion for Israel's people and their Land.

Flem set their dirty dishes in the sink then turned to Mordi. "How about a glass of port? They say a little red wine after a meal aids the digestion."

Mordi smiled. "You don't have to convince me, just lead the way."

In the sitting room, as Mordi took a seat on the sofa, Flem uncorked a bottle of his best wine. "I went to Haifa today to meet this year's quota of immigrating Jews."

"The British quota is a travesty!"

Flem nodded, handing Mordi his glass of port. "You'll get no argument out of me about that … anyway, while I was there looking for someone to interview, I met a young Jew who told me a most interesting story about his miraculous escape from a concentration camp in Romania."

"Romania!" Mordi said with a look of disgust. "That hellhole is almost as bad as Poland. Did you hear what happened there this morning? Some fascists in Lublin opened fire on a waiting room full of Jews."

Flem spilled a little of the wine he was pouring. "When is it going to end?" He pulled out his handkerchief to wipe it up.

"Wait!" Mordi said. "It gets worse. In the same district other fascists ambushed a detachment of Polish soldiers. When they found out that only two of them were Jewish, they let the rest go and shot the Jews."

Disheartened, Flem sat down in a chair across from Mordi. "It's as if the war never ended."

"It hasn't! Not in Poland. Nine Jews were kidnapped in broad daylight just last month. They dragged them into the woods and shot them. They murdered a family that was just released from Oswiecim, and in Rzeszow after some fascist spread a bunch of vicious lies about a Jew sacrificing some Christian Polish girl in a ritual, the townspeople dragged Jews out of their homes and beat them up. They would've lynched them if two of their saner citizens hadn't stopped them."

"Thank God for righteous Gentiles."

Mordi glared at Flem as if he were a moron. "Righteous? I wouldn't go that far!"

"Well, I would. Christian Danes, mostly Lutherans, risked their lives to smuggle our people out of Denmark into Sweden while we were occupied. I call that righteous."

"Yeah, well in Germany, Lutherans were busy turning Jews over to the Nazis."

Flem tried not to react, or at least not to show it. "Prejudice cuts both ways, you know. Proverbs says those who air their opinions without understanding are fools."

Mordi's jaw twitched. "Is that your way of calling me a fool, Lund?"

"I would never do that, Mordi," Flem said, careful to keep his tone modulated. "But you shouldn't paint Christians, true Christians who are part of God's remnant, with the same brush you paint hypocrites."

Mordi stood up suddenly, splashing some port on his trousers.

Glad for the distraction, Flem got up, too. "Hold on, I'll get you some peroxide and a towel."

Mordi followed close behind. "The remnant are Jews who haven't bent their knee to idols. Christians pray to statues of dead saints and their three-headed god!"

Angered by the remark, Flem handed him the peroxide. "Not all of them do."

"Well, I'm just one paper away from being ordained as a rabbi, and I disagree."

"So was my friend Katlev," Flem said, handing Mordi a towel.

"Then you better have a long talk with him."

"I wish I could, but I can't. He's dead." Knowing he'd rather read him Isaiah 48, Flem rushed out of the bathroom. But when he grabbed the Scriptures off his desk, Mordi stared at the Bible as if it were a snake about to strike.

"What are you doing with that thing?"

"Katlev challenged me to read it for myself, and it opened my eyes."

Mordi's expression dripped distain. "And you still call yourself a Jew?"

"I am a Jew, one who knows the Messiah."

Mordi set the peroxide and towel on Flem's desk. "Yeah, well, you're not the kind of Jew I like to associate with." He walked out, slamming the door behind him.

ꟹ☙

Aldur handed his landlady the rent. When she tucked it into her apron, he said, "You better count it. I paid you for three months."

"Why so much?"

"I can take two months back."

"No! Is good! Is good! Thalia keep."

Aldur smiled. "Then I'll need a receipt."

"Why? Thalia memory good, not forget."

"That's great, but I'd still like a receipt, if you don't mind."

The old woman shrugged. "Keep shirt on. Thalia give."

Aldur stuck his receipt in his wallet and grabbed his two valises.

A few minutes later, after tossing his camera case on the love seat, he went out to his private courtyard. The soothing chords of one of Chopin's nocturnes filled the air as he opened his new beach chair. Delighted by his neighbor's good taste in music, he hurried back to change into his swimming trunks.

Ten minutes later, as Aldur was about to doze off in his lounge chair, he heard what sounded like scraping. It seemed to be coming from the unit next to his. Curious as to what could be causing it, Aldur got up and peeked over the fence. An old woman with her back toward him was on her knees digging into the dirt with a small spade. Next to her, lined up in a row, were several potted plants that Aldur wasn't familiar with.

Inspired by the domesticity of the quaint scene, Aldur went in and grabbed his camera. He counted off fifteen seconds in between each snapshot, just in case the old girl hadn't lost her hearing. After his fourth, the woman turned her head sightly. But the large brim of her old-fashioned sunbonnet hid her features from him. Hoping for a close up, if she ever turned around far enough to show her profile, Aldur reached into his camera case for the lens he needed.

A minute or so later, when Aldur was about to give up and go back to sunbathing, the old lady stood up spryly and turned in his direction. He snapped her picture, mesmerized by her beauty. As she swiped at the tears streaming down her cheeks with her glove, it left a streak across her porcelain cheek.

Suddenly, Aldur felt like a voyeur. He ducked down on his side of the fence, disgusted with himself. He put his camera back into its case and went inside. But when his desire to see her lovely features again outweighed his remorse for prying, Aldur changed into his ambulance uniform. If he hurried, he might be able to find a photography studio in town that would develop his film before he had to clock in at the hospital.

ꕥ

Liesel could hardly believe that it was already Friday, March 7th. If her doctor's calculations were accurate, the child she was carrying was now in his, or maybe her, second trimester…Marlene's child would have been, also.

Liesel blinked away tears. Now was no time to get maudlin. It would only slow her down and she still had a lot to do to get ready for tonight's dinner, she reminded herself as she tied on her apron.

Then the phone began to ring.

"Would you mind answering that, Mother?" she called upstairs as she headed into the pantry. "I'm about to start baking."

A few minutes later, when Liesel walked back into the kitchen with her arms filled, her mother said, "You're not going to like this."

"Not going to?" Liesel set her supplies on the counter. "I don't like it already from the expression on your face. What happened?"

"It's what's going to happen, or I should say what's not going to happen. One of your guests isn't coming."

"Please don't tell me that Julie can't make it."

"Wrong guest," her mother said frowning.

"Flem's not coming!" Liesel said in a panic.

"Your brother isn't going to make it tonight, I'm afraid."

"What? That rat gave me his word not three days ago!"

"Now calm down, dear. Remember your condition."

Liesel fought back angry tears. How could he do this? "He lied to me, Mother!"

"It's not your brother's fault," her mother said, walking up to console her.

"Why do you always have to take up for him?" Liesel demanded.

"Will you please just listen? The driver who was scheduled to work tonight broke his leg and Aldur has to cover for him."

Hearing it, Liesel's rage evaporated, but not her disappointment. "Why did it have to be tonight?" she asked, giving in to her tears.

"Accidents aren't planned, dear. They just happen. Now cheer up! Your husband will be here soon, so dry those pretty blue eyes and start making your crust. I'm going up to change."

"Change? Into what? You look fine to me," Liesel said.

"Your son and I are going to the beach."

"The beach?" Liesel said, getting an idea. "Would you mind stopping by Aldur's on the way and tell him that I understand about tonight."

Her mother smiled. "If it'll help assuage your guilt, I would love to. Besides, I've been dying to do just that and now I can and blame you."

Eighteen

"It's me, Aldur. Open up," Deidre said, knocking. "Caleb's with me, but we won't be staying long. We're on our way to the beach."

Three seconds later, Aldur opened the door.

"Liesel asked me to drop by to let you know that she understands about tonight."

"Are you going to the beach, too, Uncle Aldur?" Caleb said, staring at his uncle's swim trunks.

"No, Caleb," he replied, ruffling the boy's curls. "I'm sunning in my courtyard. Would you like to see it?"

"We most certainly would," Deidre said maneuvering passed him. The inside of his place wasn't all that bad. Still, she would never understand why he preferred living here when he could live with them for free. Then she noticed a stack of three by five photographs.

Caleb picked them up. "Who are all these people, Uncle Aldur?"

"Hold them by the edges or you'll leave smudges," Aldur warned.

"Who are they?" Deidre asked.

Aldur shrugged. "Oh, just some faces I found interesting at the camp."

"At that Displaced Person's Camp? Really? They're mostly kids."

"Sad, isn't it? The place looked like an armed prison camp for juveniles."

"May I see them when you're finished, Caleb?" Deidre asked him.

The child handed her the stack … all except the one he kept staring at. "Why is the pretty lady crying? Did something bad happen to her at that camp, Uncle Aldur?"

Aldur sighed. "She's not from the camp, Caleb."

"You know, you've really got talent, dear," Deidre said, studying each one of them closely. Then she set them back on his desk. "I think perhaps you're in the wrong profession, Son."

"I don't have a profession, Mother. I drive an ambulance, remember?"

"I'm serious, Aldur. These are good…you should think about submitting them to a few magazines."

"Why is that lady crying?" Caleb asked, still staring at her photo.

Deidre plucked it out of the child's hands about to lay it on top of the others, then took a closer look. "Why, she's beautiful? What's her name?"

Aldur shrugged. "I have no idea, but she lives in the next bungalow."

"You should go over there and introduce yourself," Deidre told him with a playful lilt in her voice as she placed the picture on top of the others.

"Mind your business, Mother, dearest."

Deidre smiled. "You're getting quite a tan. Take care that you don't burn."

"I won't. I'm doing it gradually."

Deidre sighed. "Well, I guess I better let you get back to whatever it was you were doing and get this one," she grabbed Caleb's hand, "to the beach."

Aldur held open the door for them.

She kissed his tanned cheek then nudged Caleb. "Say goodbye to your uncle. We're off to the beach."

Caleb hung his head, frowning.

"Why the long face?" she asked, surprised by his reaction. "I thought you were in a hurry to get there."

"I am…only…"

"Only what?" Deidre insisted.

"I want to know why the lady's crying."

ഌ൦ദ

Flem tipped the cab driver generously, then turned to admire the sandstone home his in-laws had rented. Its long, narrow windows must reach nearly to the ceiling, he mused as he dropped his duffle bag next to him on the porch. After giving the door four hard raps, he waited, hoping that Liesel would be the one who opened it…and she was.

"You're early!" she exclaimed gleefully. "I didn't expect you until late this afternoon."

"I caught an earlier flight…but if you want," he teased, "you can call a cab to take me back to the airport and I'll wait a few more hours."

"I most certainly will not!"

"Then kiss me!" Flem said.

When he opened his arms, she grabbed his hand and pulled him inside. As the door shut behind them, Flem pulled his pregnant wife into his arms and kissed her hungrily for several seconds.

"I can't believe you're finally here," Liesel whispered when he finally released her.

"Where's Caleb?"

"Mother took him to the beach."

"What about your father?"

"He's still at the hospital. Why?"

"We're all alone!" he declared provocatively.

Liesel blushed. "Well, don't get any ideas. Mother and Caleb will be back any time now."

Making one of his son's pouty faces, Flem hung his head then grabbed the doorknob.

"Where are you going?" Liesel asked.

Flem smiled. "Relax, min smukke. My duffle bag is still on the porch."

"Why don't you go and freshen up, but don't be long. I'm dying to hear how it feels to be living your dream instead of writing more obituaries."

ᘓᘐ

Flem followed his nose into the kitchen, then stopped when he spotted one of his wife's pies cooling on a rack. He inhaled deeply. "Mmm…I sure have missed that aroma. Is it peach or cherry?"

"It's apple," she said. When she turned around, she gaped open-mouthed at his legs. "What in the world are you wearing, Flem? Have you joined the British Army?"

"You didn't pack me any shorts, min smukke! Roger gave me these khakis. Don't you like them?" he asked as he opened the oven. "Mmm…I knew that had to be your brisket. But where's your challah bread?" he asked, shutting the door.

"I'm letting it rise on the deck."

He took her in his arms. "Can I help you with anything?"

"You certainly can. You can sit down at the table and talk to me."

Flem smiled. "What, or I should say who do you want to hear about first? A young Jew who escaped from a concentration camp in Romania after the angel of the Lord made him invisible? Or the pompous Foreign Editor of the *Palestine Post* named Mordechai Ginzburg, who doesn't want to associate with a Jew like me?"

Liesel dropped her potato peeler on the counter with a thud. "Why not?"

"I really liked him at first. We had so much in common until Mordi made a few slurs about Christians I strongly disagreed with and I set him straight."

"You set him straight? What did you say?"

Flem sighed, then rehashed all the particulars … the good, the not so good, and the egregious. "Since then, I've done some checking. Mordechai Ginzburg is very well-connected. He could ruin my reputation if he wanted to."

"Do you think he will?" Liesel asked.

Flem shrugged. "I don't know … I certainly hope he won't."

"Well don't worry about it, Flem."

"Believe me, I'm trying not to. But sabras can get very tight-lipped when they don't trust you."

"Why wouldn't they trust you? And who are these sabras?"

"They're Jews who were born in the Land, both before and after the British took control. In Hebrew they're called tzabarim after the cactus that grows there."

"They named indigenous Jews after cactus? Isn't that anti-Semitic?"

Flem laughed. "They call themselves that, and proudly. Like the cactus, they're known for being prickly on the outside but sweet on the inside. But if they don't trust me, I can't do my job."

"Of course, you can! You're a great journalist, Flem." She took hold of his hands. "Have you already forgotten?"

"That I'm a journalist? Of course not!"

Liesel smiled. "No, silly. Don't you remember? You told me, the Lord told you that He'd turn your defeats into victories."

Flem relaxed. "You're amazing, min smukke! Do you know that?" He pulled her onto his lap then placed his hand lovingly on her abdomen.

Liesel smiled. "This is the first day of our daughter's second trimester."

"Our daughter's?"

"She's a girl … at least I hope so," Liesel said, getting up.

"Well, I'll be happy either way," he told her as she went back to peeling her potatoes. "So long as our baby's healthy."

"Aldur's child would have been close to the same age."

"Don't torture yourself, min smukke. How's your brother getting on these days anyway?"

"He rented a bungalow near here earlier this week."

"Well good for him! He's moving on with his life."

Liesel stopped peeling and turned around. "He was supposed to join us tonight, but now he has to cover for another driver who broke his leg."

"Well, don't worry. We can go visit him tomorrow or invite him here."

"But you don't understand. I also invited Julie Abercrombie."

"Is Roger coming, too?" Flem asked.

When his wife shook her head as if she'd lost her best friend, Flem grew suspicious. "Why do I get the feeling there's more to this than you're telling me?"

"I just wanted them to meet! That's all!"

"No, it isn't! Don't lie to me!" Flem got up, took the peeler out of her hand and laid it on the counter. "What you want is for the two of them to fall madly in love. Admit it!"

"So, what if I do? They're perfect for each other, Flem!"

"How can you say that? You've never laid eyes on her."

"But you have, and you told me yourself that she's beautiful. She's also a Christian Aldur's age…and they're both grieving."

"And that makes them a perfect match?" Flem wanted to laugh. "I'm afraid you've been reading too many romance novels, min smukke."

"Oh, stop it, Flem! I've only read three in my entire life. But I do know my brother a lot better than you do. And I want him to be happy…not alone!"

"Aldur isn't alone. He's got you. He's got your folks. He's got me and all of his friends back home."

"It's not the same, Flem."

"You need to give him some time to grieve, min smukke." When her eyes began to moisten, Flem pulled her into his arms. Then his mother-in-law strolled into the kitchen and removed her beach hat.

Liesel looked at her and gasped. "Is Caleb sunburned, too?"

"He's fine. He's upstairs. It's good to see you again, Flem. You look well, I must say. Now come give you mother-in-law a hug."

"Well, you certainly don't look well, Mother. You look like you need to be doused with a gallon of vinegar."

"She's right," Flem said as he embraced her gingerly. "You should put something on that burn or you'll be miserable tonight."

"How can Caleb be just fine, Mother? You look like a boiled lobster!"

"Skin doesn't burn when it's buried under sand."

"Why did Caleb bury himself in the sand?" Liesel asked.

"The little monkey's been in a foul mood all afternoon."

"Why?" Liesel insisted.

"Oh, he's obsessed about some photograph Aldur took. Your brother really is talented," Deidre said grabbing an apple out of the basket. "You should consider hiring him if you're ever looking for a photographer, Flem."

"Why is he obsessed over a photograph?" Liesel asked.

When Deidre rolled her eyes and took a bite of her apple instead of answering Liesel's question, she stripped off her apron. "Forget it, Mother. I'll go up and ask him myself."

"I wouldn't if I were you," Deidre warned. "Not unless you're prepared to explain to him why the pretty lady in the photograph was crying."

Nineteen

"Your place is lovely, Liesel," Julie said, following her hostess. The high ceiling reminded her of all those English manor homes she and her brother had toured when they were in school.

"Excuse me, everyone," Liesel said as they entered the parlor. "Our guest of honor has finally arrived. Please make her feel welcome while I go finish up a few things in the kitchen."

Flem walked up to her first and took her hand. "It's so good to see you again, Julie. You left so suddenly I never got an opportunity to say goodbye."

"I apologize for that, Flem. It's just…well—"

"You've no need to explain. Roger already has. Healing takes time."

Julie sighed. "I certainly have plenty of that, don't I?"

"If that's the case," Dr. Prestur said, smiling as he extended his arm to her, "I can have your supervisor give you more shifts."

Julie smiled.

"My spies at the hospital have given me some glowing reports about you, Nurse Abercrombie. Compassion, these days, is a rare commodity."

"Thank you, Doctor, and please call me Julie since we're not at the hospital."

"Only if you call me Juhl," he said as an attractive woman with a ghastly sunburn offered Julie her hand.

"Welcome to our home, Julie. I'm Deidre Prestur—Liesel's mother and this one's wife," she said, elbowing Juhl's side.

"It's wonderful to finally get to meet you, all of you. And I hope you're treating that burn."

"Can't you smell all the vinegar? Liesel practically baptized me in it as soon as I got home."

"Well just be sure to cover up when you go out. You don't want to make it worse," Julie advised.

Deidre studied her closely. "Have we met somewhere before? You look so familiar."

"Not that I know of," Julie said.

Deidre led her over to one of the sofas. "Now sit down and tell me all about yourself."

Julie forced a smile. "With all that's going on in this world, I'm sure we can find something more interesting to talk about."

"Oh, I don't believe that for one minute. A beautiful creature like you? Surely, there must be some dashing young man in your life."

"There was once … but he died."

"I'm so sorry," Deidre said. "Were the two of you engaged?"

"Not yet, we weren't."

"Asher was a sabra," Flem said, saving Julie the painful explanation. "He was a member of the Hagenah and was critically burned recently in an Arab attack on one of our settlements."

"So, your young man was Jewish?"

Julie bristled. "Is that a problem?"

"No! Of course not. I just thought…oh well…never mind."

"You just thought what?" Julie insisted.

"Well, you're a Christian, so I thought…"

"Asher knew his Messiah, knew Him better than most Christians I've met, and I wish everyone would just…" Regretting her tone, Julie stopped mid-sentence. "Please forgive me," she said, looking around at all the stunned faces. "I didn't mean to attack you like that,

Deidre. Maybe, I should leave."

Julie started to get up, but Deidre grabbed her hand. "Please don't go! I'm the one who should be apologizing…and I do. Please stay."

"Yes, Julie," Dr. Prestur said. "I'm sure you took my wife's remark the wrong way. After all, our son-in-law is Jewish and a believer."

"I'll pour you some wine," Flem offered, heading over to the bar.

Julie nodded appreciatively as Deidre patted her hand. "Our son, Aldur, lost his wife recently, too."

"And the child she was carrying," Dr. Prestur added. "So, we know the pain you're going through."

Flem handed her the wine. "The heart takes time to heal, but it will."

"All of you have my condolences … and Aldur, too," Julie said in an attempt to refocus their conversation.

"If he hadn't been called into work tonight, you could've given him your condolences yourself," Deidre told her.

"Does Aldur live here with you?"

Deidre frowned. "Not anymore. He just moved into one of those dreary little cottages near the beach."

Julie hung her head. Determined not to take offense, she forced a smile. "They are dreary. Aren't they?"

"You know the place?" Deidre asked.

"Oh, yes, I certainly do. I live in one of them."

Deidre gasped, turning an even deeper shade of red. "I'm so sorry, Julie. I didn't mean to—"

"You've no need to apologize, Deidre. They are dreary. Still, dreary or not, I prefer it there to being billeted in a dormitory filled with nurses whose life goal is to party every night. There, at least, I have some privacy."

"Excuse me, everyone," Liesel said, interrupting her. "Dinner's finally ready, so why don't you all go into the dining room while I get my son. The poor boy's had a trying day, so I fed him earlier, but Flem and I want him with us for the Sabbath liturgy."

Glad for the distraction, Julie stood up first.

Flem led her into the dining room. The elegantly set table had little place cards on every plate with each of their names. Julie was still looking around for hers when Liesel returned with her son. The bashful little fellow—though precious to behold—seemed as reluctant to be there as Julie felt.

Liesel nudged the boy forward. "Caleb, greet our guests."

The child drooped his head. "Shabbat shalom," he said in a tiny voice.

"You can do better than that, young man," Flem told him. "Now greet our guest properly."

Caleb lifted his head. But the second the boy's gaze met Julie's, his pouty angelic face lit up.

As the child ran over to her, Deidre gasped. "That's why I recognized you!"

"What do you mean?" Julie demanded.

"You're the lady in my son's photographs," Deidre explained.

Caleb tugged on Julie's skirt. "Why were you crying?"

"What are you all talking about?" Julie demanded, feeling as if she were acting out a surreal scene in some nightmare.

"You were gardening, and my son—"

"I'm sure Aldur meant you no harm," Liesel cried, interrupting her mother's explanation.

But Julie would not be deterred. "What did Aldur do?"

"He snapped a few pictures," Deidre said. "In one of them you were crying."

Julie's eyes filled with tears. She turned to Liesel. "I'm sorry, but I can't stay. Not after all this."

Liesel followed her into the hallway. "Please give us another chance, Julie. It's the Sabbath after all, and we're supposed to forgive. I want to be your friend."

Julie spun around. "Well, I wanted Asher to live but he's dead. So don't try and manipulate me with what the Bible says."

Liesel grabbed her hand. "Can't you at least pray about it?"

"Pray? To a God I can't trust?"

"What about Asher? Can you trust him?"

"Asher is dead!" Julie said as tears streamed down her cheeks.

"So is Katlev, but he's still alive in my husband's heart."

"I want Asher alive in my arms."

As she turned to leave, Liesel stopped her. "If you really want Asher to be more than a fading memory, there's only one way to make it happen, Julie."

"Of course, I want that."

"Then consider what Asher would advise you to do at this moment and do it."

Twenty

The next morning, three succinct raps rattled Aldur's door. He sat up in bed and rubbed his eyes. Then the insistent knocking started up again. "Keep your shirt on! I'm coming," he yelled, snatching his bathrobe off the foot of his hide-a-bed.

"Take your time, old buddy. It's only us."

"Well, it's awfully early to be socializing, Flem. I worked last night," he complained, opening the door.

"I wanted to make sure we saw you first," his sister explained, darting past him.

Aldur stifled a yawn. "Saw me first?"

Liesel blushed then turned to her husband.

Flem raised both hands. "Don't look at me! This was your idea, Liesel. I just came along to keep the peace, remember?"

Aldur shut the door. "It's too early for riddles, you two! I haven't had coffee yet."

Flem smiled at him apologetically and clapped his arm. "Then you better go make some, old buddy. You're going to need it."

"What's that supposed to mean?" Aldur asked.

"This place isn't half bad," Flem said. "I'm surprised your mother hates it."

"I'll make the coffee and let you and Flem talk. Just show me where everything is."

"You're changing our game plan, min smukke."

"Please, Flem…"

"Alright … but you'll owe me one."

"Owe you one what?" Aldur asked him.

"Why don't you show me around first? Then I'll tell you more than you want to know."

"More than I want to know?"

"Let it go, old buddy. Ignorance is bliss."

Aldur shrugged. "If you say so, but there's not much to show that you're not already looking at except my parcel of desert out back. Want to see it?"

"No!" Liesel shouted as one of his landlady's porcelain cups shattered at his sister's feet. "Sorry! It slipped."

"Look, you two, my gut tells me I'm not going to like whatever it is you came here to tell me, so let's just bite the bullet and get it over with?"

"Tell him, Flem. I'll clean up my mess and make us coffee."

Aldur shoved his bed into the wall then plopped into an armchair.

Flem took the loveseat. "Remember that photograph you took, the one with the lady crying?"

"How do you know about that?"

"That was Julie Abercrombie."

Aldur sat up straight. "Why didn't my mother tell me?"

"She didn't know, not until last night."

Aldur dropped his head between his hands and groaned.

"Caleb recognized her. According to your mother, he was obsessed … your mother's words, not mine."

"Obsessed with what?" Aldur asked.

"With why, and I quote, was the pretty lady crying?"

Aldur slumped back into his chair, wishing it were a sink hole.

"I'm sure now she wishes she'd made something up to satisfy Caleb's curiosity, but she didn't."

"I told him he should pray and ask the Lord," Liesel explained, joining in the conversation from the kitchen.

"Do you want to tell him the rest, Liesel, or shall I?"

"You better do it, Flem. I don't want to drop any more of his dishes."

Aldur groaned. "Please don't tell me this is going to get worse."

"Okay, old buddy, I won't...but it does...much worse."

Aldur forced himself to sit up and take his medicine like a man. "Then let's get this over with. At least that way I'll know what I'm dealing with."

"Things didn't get too rocky until your mother mentioned that you'd just moved into, and again I'm quoting her, one of those dreary little cottages near the beach. When Julie explained that she lived in one of them, you should've seen your mother's face. It turned a deep purple under her sunburn," Flem said, then went on to lay out every embarrassing detail of last night's disastrous Shabbat dinner.

By the time Liesel brought in their coffee, Aldur direly needed caffeine, needed it strong and undiluted. So, he passed on his usual cream and sugar as Liesel picked up with her part of the story.

"For a second there, after I told her to consider what Asher would advise, I thought Julie might stay." Liesel shrugged. "But she didn't."

Flem patted his wife's hand. "It was good advice just the same. It's just too bad Julie failed to take it."

"But I have to confess," Liesel said, "I know exactly how she feels. I struggled with anger at God, too, after Marlene's death. Didn't I, Flem?"

"For a while, but you got over it."

"You're the one who surprised me, Aldur. Your faith never faltered."

Aldur sighed. "I knew where that would lead, and like I told you that night, I won't go there again."

Flem leaned forward with a glint in his eye. "Then you're the one, old buddy, who needs to reach out to Julie."

"Me? She hates me! I'm the voyeur, remember?"

"But Aldur, don't you see?" Liesel said. "Julie needs to learn to trust again. And who better than you can teach her that?"

"Your sister's right. Julie's fighting the battle you've already won."

"Who knows?" Liesel said. "Maybe, just maybe, it wasn't the Tempter who put you up to snapping Julie's picture."

"What are you talking about?" Aldur asked.

Flem smiled. "What if it was Yeshua?"

ꙮ

Julie placed the Taylors of Harrogate Breakfast Tea her cousin Helen sent her the month before back in the cupboard, then shut it with a sigh. The endearing words Helen had inscribed on the birthday card that came with it were all lies now. She wasn't winsome, wasn't cheerful, and certainly not trusting! How could she be after Asher's unnecessary death? And last night's episode made matters worse. Now she couldn't even take her morning tea in her own courtyard, thanks to that odious voyeur in the unit next to hers. As she opened a fresh tin of crumpets, she came to a decision. On her next day off, she would start looking for another place to live. Only, it would have to be close to the hospital, and that wouldn't be easy to find, not in her price range. As Julie was about to bite into her crumpet someone knocked at her door.

"Who is it?" she grumpily demanded. Then remembering that Thalia had promised to stop by and fix her dripping faucet, she quickly added, in a much friendlier tone, "Coming. Be right there." But when she opened it, a tall, fair-haired man in his twenties flashed her a sheepish grin.

"I hope I'm not disturbing you, Miss Abercrombie. I'm Aldur Prestur, Fleming Lund's brother-in-law, and I'd like to—"

Horrified, she slammed the door, or tried to at least, but his foot got in the way.

Aldur winced. "I only came over to say I'm sorry."

Stricken by her cruelty, she glanced down to assess the damage. "You're bleeding."

Aldur smiled weakly. "Guess I shouldn't have tried using my foot as a door stop."

"That is but one of many things you should never have done."

"I really am sorry. As soon as I saw your face, I put away my camera."

"You never should've gotten it out in the first place."

"You're right. And I apologize. I wasn't thinking. In that bonnet and gardening apron you…well, the truth is, I thought you were an elderly lady."

"An old lady? Oh, I see, and that I suppose justifies not only invading my privacy but photographing me, too?"

"No! That's not what I meant. Seeing you gardening on your knees was a Norman Rockwell moment, and I gave in to it. But I promise you, it will never happen again. The second I saw your tears, I—"

"Snapped my picture!" she said, having dealt with smooth talkers before.

Aldur frowned. "No. I was about to say, 'loathed myself.'"

"If that were true you wouldn't have developed the film. But you did!"

"There were other pictures on the roll."

"Women in bathing suits, I presume," she said, eyeing his tan.

"Teenagers from the camp."

"You took pictures at the D.P. Camp?"

"That place is a horror!" Aldur said, looking as if he meant it. "I had no idea it would be that bad."

"Neither does most of the world," Julie lamented.

"My mother thinks I should send them to a few magazines."

"That's a wonderful idea! But I'd ask Flem to write an article to submit with them. Your photos will carry more weight that way." She glanced down at the blood trickling from his little toe onto her mat. "Why don't you come in and let me bandage that?" she asked, realizing that Aldur wasn't quite the cad she'd imagined him to be. "You don't want it to get infected."

Aldur grinned. "Is that your way of saying I'm forgiven?"

Julie hesitated. "Let's just say it's my way of doing good to someone who despitefully used me."

"Ouch!" Aldur said, bringing a smile to her lips.

"Well?" She opened her door wider. "Are you coming in, or aren't you?"

ꕥ

"Inspired by your green thumb, I picked up some shrubs the other day," Aldur told Julie as she led him into her kitchen. "How's that garden of yours growing?"

Julie sighed. "It needs to be watered. I keep forgetting I'm not in England anymore." She pulled out a chair for him to sit. "Did your wife have a green thumb?"

"I don't know—we lived in an apartment—but my mother certainly does."

Julie set a canister on the table. "That's a rather nasty burn she has. She'll need to keep out of the sun until it heals."

"She must've burned after dropping by yesterday. Oh, well, that only goes to prove that old adage."

"What old adage is that?" Julie asked.

"The one that says we teach best that which we need to learn."

Julie laughed as she draped a towel over her lap. "Well, don't tease her too much. Now give me that foot."

Aldur slipped off his sandal.

"Well, what are you waiting for?" she asked.

"You sure you want to do this?"

Julie smiled. "I do it all the time. Don't you trust me?"

"Of course," he said, then watched in silence as she washed then painted his little toe with a stinging antiseptic that turned it purple and burned like the dickens. But the truth was he rather enjoyed it and was sorry when she finished.

"Keep the bandage on until tomorrow morning at least."

"And after that?" he asked, slipping his foot back into his sandal.

Julie flashed him a mischievous grin. "You'll need to keep away from slamming doors!"

"Touché!" he said, laughing.

They were both quiet, just smiling at each other after that. When the silence between them grew embarrassing, Aldur stood up, not wanting to go. "Guess I'd better let you get back to whatever you were doing before I, shall we say, put my foot in it?"

Julie smiled and walked him to the door. The moment it closed, Aldur hurried back to his place and rummaged through his desk. With pen in hand, he wrote: May these be put to use by the girl with the green thumb who knows more about growing things than I ever will. He signed it, Your devoted and contrite neighbor, Aldur.

A few minutes later, having arranged all of his potted plants in a semicircle in front of Julie's door, Aldur stuck his note in an envelope. Then he placed it over the bloodstain on her doormat and went back to his bungalow humming chords from Chopin's Nocturne in E flat.

ꕥ

On March 15th, a week after his weekend in Cyprus, Flem returned to his apartment frustrated that all his efforts to locate the young Romanian had failed. Then he saw the eviction notice taped to his door. It was signed by his landlord, Elias Eskolski and gave him exactly one week to vacate the premises, no explanation given.

But Flem didn't need one. He knew what, or rather who, caused it and gave into a moment of anger. Then the Holy Ruach reminded him that all things work together for good to those who love God and are called according to His purpose. Releasing a heavy sigh, Flem resolved to do what the good book said and count it all joy. Tonight, he'd go to bed early—he was really beat—and in the morning, after spending time with the Lord, he'd grab some breakfast in the Old City then take a cab over to the Goldbergs' to see if their offer of Jacob's old room was still good.

ꕥ

On March 20th, unable to take on a single bunker of fuel in Norfolk, due to a fuel crisis, the *Warfield* set sail for Paulsboro on the Delaware, where an old confidant of Captain Ash's assured him they could purchase all the fuel they would need to make it into the Azores. From Cape Charles to Henlopen, the old barge glided through the ocean with ease, but when she hit the Delaware's breakwaters, her superstructure began exhibiting what the Navy referred to as an exaggerated streetcar effect.

"I am not making any more repairs!" Captain Ash yelled at his first mate as several anxious looking crew members gathered around to listen. "Our underwriters, even the classification society, has declared the *Warfield* seaworthy."

"Her housing's been stiffened, Captain, but it didn't eliminate her sway."

"Sway or no sway, this ship's insured by Lloyds of London! And I'm not spending one more dime!"

"Begging your pardon, Captain," one of his new crewmembers said, "if she's so seaworthy, why is Captain Johnson taking over for you?"

"Because we've wasted too much time here, not to mention money. If we hadn't, we'd be in France by now. But we're not, and I have prior commitments I can't get out of. So, stop your insulting insinuations. Just shut up or get off my ship!"

Those gathered exchanged angry looks. Then one by one, they walked off the bride, all except Bernie, his first mate. "Well, what do you want?" Ash demanded.

"What about taking her outside territorial waters, Captain, then bracing her superstructure with wiring cable and turnbuckles ourselves?"

"If *by ourselves* you mean this crew, you must be nuts! These clowns aren't seamen enough!"

ജ്ജ

Early that next morning, Captain Ash set course for the *Warfield*'s final stateside docking, a lay birth in Philadelphia at the foot of South Street where a new problem slapped him across the face.

"I understand that, Captain Ash, but your ship carries a foreign registry. And the regulations say you have to deposit her papers as soon as you enter port."

"I know, but this is Saturday. Your Customs House is closed!"

"Then pay the fine."

Ash gritted his teeth, now fully convinced that the *Warfield* was jinxed. "How much?"

"If you're here before noon Monday, it'll cost you $1,000, but one minute after that you'll have to add another five hundred."

"What time does the Customs House open?"

"At 9:00 a.m. sharp."

"I'll see you at 9:30 then," the captain said and stormed out, but his problems had only just begun.

As soon as he stepped off the gangway onto the jinxed *Warfield*, Bernie came running up to him. "We've got a problem, Captain."

"Only one? Let's celebrate," he said, sarcastically.

"Actually, five, sir."

"Five what?" he said, in no mood to play games.

"Five of the six new crewmembers you ordered to shut up or get off the ship yesterday, well, they did, sir. They packed their foot lockers and called a cab."

"This cursed ship is gonna be the death of me yet!"

"Replacing all of them with adequately trained sailors will take, at bare minimum, another week."

And it did.

But in the end, the added days proved to be beneficial for two of their newest replacements were experienced sailors, and one, a young fella named Frank Stanzac, became the *Warfield*'s second non-Jewish crewmember.

ϪϹϚ

By the end of that week the atmosphere aboard ship had brightened. With the warmer rays promising that summer was near, Captain Ash's temper cooled. Tickled that he'd soon be rid of the old *Warfield* and all of her jinxes for good, he accepted a call from the consul general of Honduras, Manuel Funes, gleefully. "Ola, my friend. How's life been treating you these days?"

"Our Embassy has reason to believe that Marseille won't be your final destination."

Ash stopped smiling. "Says who?"

"The British Embassy. Our ambassador is sending me to Philadelphia. He's instructed me to pull your ship's registry … and flag."

Ash began to sweat. He had to think fast. "What train will you be taking?"

"Why?" Funes asked, sounding suspicious.

"Well, I'd like to go with you."

"Really? You're not going to pitch one of your fits?"

"Who me?" the captain asked, smiling again, for he knew that every Saturday Lavina Shipping closed at noon.

"Okay then," Funes said, sounding more relaxed. "How soon can you meet me at Penn Station?"

"Oh, by 10:30 I'm sure," Ash told him. "Why don't we meet up at the information desk?"

"Well, don't be late!"

"I won't, Consul General," Ash assured him. He hung up then dialed the *Warfield*'s agent. "I need to send a message to Captain Johnson right away. Tell him he's to board the crew now!"

"Why now?" Dewitt asked.

"Don't argue with me, man, just do it! Oh, and be sure to tell Johnson that I'll be giving him a bonus for every fifteen minutes before noon they're out of there. Got it?"

"Will do, Captain. Over and out."

ꕥ

Ash and Funes boarded a train bound for North Philadelphia at 10:45 a.m. When they reached Lavina Shipping at 1:00 p.m., the door was locked.

Ash feigned disappointment. "Well, don't worry, Manuel. The *Warfield*'s docked on South Street. So why don't we grab us some lunch at the Bellevue-Stratford then head over there and I'll pull down your flag myself."

"Well, I am getting hungry."

Ash smiled. "Good! Then what are we waiting for?"

ꙮ

When they arrived at the dock at 3:15, the *Warfield* wasn't there.

"Excuse me," Ash said to one of the sailors passing by on the pier. "Any idea when the *Warfield* pulled out?"

"A little after eleven this morning, I think, maybe a quarter after."

"Thanks," Ash told him then turned to Manuel.

Funes stared back at Ask, looking fit to be tied.

Ash clasped his arm. "We tried!"

"You expect me to tell that to my ambassador?"

"Relax! I promise you I'll wire Captain Johnson just as soon as the ship docks in Marseille and instruct him to switch our registry to Panama…money talks over there. When the *Warfield* leaves France, you can guarantee your ambassador she won't be flying a Honduran flag."

Twenty-One

Thirteen days later, in the early morning on April 5,1947, after pitching and swaying halfway across the Atlantic, Captain Johnson came to a decision. If his crew could laugh off all the ship's creaking and groaning, he might as well too. Ash's rants about the *Warfield* being jinxed were nothing but rubbish. That, of course, happened before Captain Johnson took a patched-in call from Ben Saade.

"You can't dock at Horta!"

"We have to! We're low on fuel! It's the closest bunker on our route."

"I work under a British franchise, remember? They're furious that you slipped out of their clutches in Philadelphia...the Portuguese are after you too. So, head for Ponta Delgada while I try to figure out a solution."

ꙮ

Two hours later, critically low on fuel, the *Warfield* moored at the far end of a quay in Ponta Delgada used for loading and unloading. When the off-watch crew went ashore to sample the town's bistros, John Bark headed for his cabin to pray for a solution.

Steven Greenbaum stopped him. "Have you seen the captain?"

"He was on his way to the galley. Why? What's happened now?"

Steven pointed to a Norwegian ship starboard of the *Warfield*. "See that freighter? I just spoke to their captain. He said we could pump all the oil we need from cement tanks on the pier. But we'll have to bribe the guards and do it at night, of course."

"You mean pinch it?" John asked, appalled.

"Why not? It's been done before according to their skipper."

"Well, we can't do it. It's against the eighth commandment: Thou shalt not steal."

Greenburg turned red. "You got a better idea? Ah, forget it! It's the captain I need to talk to not some holier than thou preacher."

John went back to his cabin, but instead of praying his usual way, he reached for his Bible. "Speak to me. I need Your wisdom." Trusting that the Lord would lead him to the right page, he opened the book without looking then began to read.

Joshua the son of Nun secretly sent two men from Shittim as spies. "Go view the land, especially Jericho," he told them. They went into the house of a prostitute named Rahab and lodged there. When it was told to the king of Jericho, "Behold, men of Israel have come here tonight to search out the land," the king of Jericho sent men to Rahab. "Bring out the men who entered your house. They came here to search out our land."

But the woman, who hid them said, "True, those men came to me, but I did not know where they were from and when the gate was about to close at dark, they went out, and I know not where."

Confused, John shut the book. Bearing false witness was sin. Yet even the book of Hebrews in the New Testament listed Rahab among heroes of the faith.

When John shut his eyes to pray, someone pounded on his cabin door. "Captain Johnson wants everyone in the galley, pronto!"

ꟾ

"Get ready!" Captain Johnson excitedly told those he'd managed to round up. "We're shipping out tomorrow, before dawn."

"Did Ben Saade work some miracle?" his first mate asked.

"We don't need one," Greenbaum yelled back. "We'll be pumping the fuel ourselves."

John Bark jumped up. "You mean steal it, don't you?"

"Pipe down, Reverend. We're not stealing anything," Captain Johnson assured him. "I'll wire the cost as soon as we dock in France. Now, here's my plan: Greenbaum and Bernstein will bribe the guards."

"What about our crewmembers ashore?" Bernie asked.

"Any teetotalers in here?" the captain asked.

When three men sheepishly raised their hands, the captain smiled. "I need you to go round them up. I want everyone back on board and sober before dark. Any questions?" No one responded. "Good! Now scram! We've got a job to do."

ᜳ

When Flem returned that afternoon, Devorah greeted him at the door. "You'll never guess what happened today, who Mati talked to for over an hour and will be joining us for supper tonight."

"Who?" Flem asked, heading into the kitchen for a cold drink.

"Who have you been looking for?"

"Looking for?" Noting the gleam in her eyes, Flem stopped in his tracks. "Are you telling me that Mati found Yehuda?"

"Actually, Flem, it was the other way around. Your young Romanian," she said, removing a tumbler from her cupboard, "found Mati."

"Really?"

"And guess what? The boy is one of us!"

Flem smiled. "I knew it … I could see it in his eyes."

Looking delighted, she filled the glass with water and handed it to him. "Jacob was right, you know. Elohim is indeed a Dot Connector!"

"Why was Yehuda looking for Mati? Do they know each other?"

Devorah shook her head. "Eliezer sent him."

"Who's Eliezer?"

"A very precious friend of ours, and a tzadik. When he learned that Yehuda had sprained his wrist the day he arrived, he went over to pray for him as soon as he got out of the hospital."

"So, they knew each other?"

"Not then, but Eliezer always visits settlements when new Jews arrive. He likes to make sure they have what they need."

"So that's why Yehuda never got a hold of me. Well, go on, Devorah. I'm intrigued."

She flashed him a sly smile. "For now, that's all you need to know, Flem. Yehuda and Eliezer will fill you in on the details at supper tonight."

ᘓᘐ

As Flem checked his watch for the third time, Matityahu poured a glass of his wife's Moscato and handed it to him. "Here. It'll help you relax."

"I haven't felt this anxious about anything since my son was born."

"Well, it's all about timing, Flem. Elohim's timing, not ours."

Then the knock they'd all been waiting for shook the front door.

"I'll get it," Devorah called out from the kitchen.

Flem set his wine on the sideboard then dashed into the hallway with Mati following close behind. Three seconds later, they all nearly collided. When Devorah held her hand out like a traffic cop, Flem smiled. Mati scowled.

Nonchalantly she tucked a flyaway hair back under her head-covering and opened the door calmly. "Shalom! Come in! There's someone here eager to greet you."

"It's so good to see you again," Flem told the youth as he stepped over the Goldbergs' threshold. Then Flem noticed the man standing behind him, and his mouth fell open.

"Shalom, Fleming. We were bound to meet again, only I had no idea it would be this soon."

"You two know each other?" Devorah asked.

"Eliezer never gave me his name," Flem explained, "only details about a story I was covering before he …"

"Before he what?" she asked when he failed to complete his sentence.

He turned to Eliezer. "Why don't you tell them?"

The old man smiled. "Why should I when you're doing such an excellent job? By all means, continue, Fleming."

Uneasy about it, he complied. "Well, my pen ran out of ink, and by the time I dug another one out of my satchel, Eliezer was gone."

"Like Adonai's angel!" Yehuda exclaimed excitedly.

Eliezer smiled. "Well, I can assure all of you that I'm merely flesh and blood."

"Why don't we go into the dining room?" Devorah said, looking a bit nervous. "Everything is ready."

"With Elohim, many strange happenings. Yes, Flem?"

"That's one way to put it," he told the lad.

"I don't know about strange," Devorah said, "but Elohim is certainly a dot connector."

"What means dot connector?" Yehuda asked.

"Haven't you ever filled in one of those connect-the-dots puzzles in the newspaper?" Mati asked the boy, who then turned to Eliezer.

"When go home, you show Yehuda puzzle? Yes?"

"There's no need to wait," Mati said. "I've got a stack of old newspapers on my desk."

Devorah smiled. "Yes, and if I didn't sneak a few of them into the trash on a regular basis, they'd be all over the floor by now."

"My wife likes to exaggerate, Yehuda. But let's eat before her brisket gets cold and she gets hot under the collar."

"What means hot under the collar?"

Mati smiled. "I'll explain that idiom to you in my office later."

After Mati's traditional berakah blessing over the food, everyone unfolded their napkins and began to eat.

Then Devorah turned to Flem. "So, tell us, how did you two dots get connected?"

"You mean me and Eliezer?" he asked, hoping she meant something else.

"Of course," she said. "We already know how you met Yehuda."

"Well…after the Officers Club got blown up," he said, speaking slowly so he could choose his words wisely, "I had to write about it. Only, sabras, as you know, can be very tightlipped when they want to be…and they wanted to be that day. I couldn't get a single soul to talk about anything until Eliezer showed up and…"

"Well, go on," Devorah urged him.

"It's all right," Eliezer said. "You can tell them, Fleming."

"He gave me all the details."

"All the details?" Mati turned to his old friend. "How could you?"

"Let Fleming finish his story. If you still have questions after that, I'll be glad to answer them."

Flem took a breath, sorry that he wasn't yet off the hook. "I asked Eliezer why he was being so forthcoming."

"And what did I answer you?"

"You told me that I'd know what to do with it."

"And did you?" the old man asked.

Flem stared down at his brisket. "Well, the truth is I never submitted it."

"And why not?" Eliezer insisted.

Flem looked him in the eye. "I didn't feel right about it, so I burned it."

Eliezer beamed. "Ah! Then I was correct, wasn't I, Fleming? You did know what to do with it."

"But why? What was the point? And how did you know? Were you part of—"

"The operation? No. Let's just say I'm very well-connected."

"Well, if you never wanted me to publish the story," he said, still disquieted by the entire episode, "why did you give me all those details?"

Eliezer beamed then started clapping his hands slowly. "Ah!

Adonai's correspondent has finally asked the only relevant question."

"Adonai's correspondent? What are you talking about?"

"I did it, Fleming, because the Ruach instructed me to. And I learned quite a long time ago not to argue but obey."

Flem smiled. "A dear friend of mine once told me nearly the same thing."

"Katlev Hertzog?" Eliezer asked.

"You knew him?"

"I never had the pleasure, but Matityahu told me all about him and Jacob years ago."

"Why did you call me Adonai's correspondent? I work for the *Gazette*."

"Because Adonai has a mission for you … and for Yehuda," he said, patting the lad's hand.

"What mission?" Flem asked as his heart began to race again.

"Are you familiar with the Aliyah Beit?"

"What Jew isn't?"

"Well, sometime this summer, should you accept the Lord's call, you and Yehuda here will board one of their ships."

"Why? I'm no sailor, and I already have a work visa."

"You need only to take notes and later you can write your articles, Fleming. Are you interested?"

"Of course! Which ship will we be on?"

"By the time you board, her name will have been changed to the *Exodus 1947*. You and Yehuda are to embark in France when they take on refugees."

Twenty-Two

ust off the coast of Gibraltar, nearing sunset on April 9th, Captain Johnson gave an order for the engines to be shut off.

"Why are we stopping, Captain?" John asked, surprised.

"Hopefully, these gusts off Africa will die down at sunset."

"And what if they don't?" John pressed him.

"Then they don't!" the captain retorted brusquely. "After dark, we'll start moving."

"But we've made it through worse gales than these. Why waste time for something that might never happen?"

"What are you babbling about, Reverend?"

"About you turning off the engines hoping the gusts might die down," he replied, struggling to keep his tone respectful.

"You blockheads, I'm waiting for dark not the wind to die down. See that rock over there?" He pointed toward Gibraltar. "I don't want whatever British frigate might be lurking around it to give chase."

John hung his head. "Sorry, Captain. I misunderstood."

"Well, go misunderstand somewhere else! I don't have time for any more of your stupid questions."

ꕥ

Twenty minutes later, Captain Johnson ordered the engines to be turned back on and every light aboard the ship turned off until they were beyond reach of the Royal Navy on their tail. After that, sailing was peaceful through the Golfe du Lion. Early that next morning, the ship moored alongside the Quai Grulet, shrouded in fog.

"You're coming with me," Captain Johnson ordered John as he was about to grab some breakfast in the galley.

"What's going on?"

"The Hagenah patched through a call a few minutes ago. They want you with me when we have our meeting this morning."

"Me? What for?"

"You can ask them that yourself. Now hurry up," he said, looking perturbed. "They're waiting for us on the dock."

A few minutes later, the more commanding of the two figures extended his arm to the captain. "I'm Joe Baharlia, your ship chandler."

Captain Johnson shook it heartily. "It's an honor to finally meet you. You and your brother are Hagenah legends."

"Keep your voice down," the man next to Baharlia warned before offering his hand to the captain. "I'll be your Hagenah agent while you're in Marseille. The name's Genista."

"This is the Reverend John Bark, our lone Gentile," the captain explained.

"Begging your pardon, Captain," John said, "but you're forgetting Frank Stanzac. There are two of us now."

"Bucky Rabinowitz speaks quite highly of you," Genista said, shaking John's hand firmly.

"Who's Rabinowitz?" the captain asked.

Genista smiled. "One of our very best procurement officers. Your man of the cloth isn't just a volunteer. Bucky head-hunted personally."

"Why?" Captain Johnson asked, looking mystified.

Baharlia clapped his arm. "Why don't we continue this in my

office. It's more private there and we can talk freely."

"But we haven't had breakfast yet," the captain complained.

The ship chandler draped his massive arm over the captain's shoulder. "We have a bistro right down the street. My secretary will run over there and order whatever you two want."

ꕥ

"We're sending you to Paris," Genista told John as he snatched up the last of the croissants.

"Why?" John asked.

"You're our liaison with the French government. Ever heard of a man named Chaim Arlosoroff?"

"I don't think so," John said.

"Chaim headed the Jewish Agency's political department until '33 when he got plugged on a beach in Tel Aviv. His daughter, Shulamet, heads up our Paris headquarters and will be working with you."

"Doing what?" John asked, still confused.

"British Intelligence and the Sûreté see very little difference between Irgun, the Stern Group, and the Hagenah."

"Who are the Sûreté?" John asked.

"France's Criminal Investigative Department. They're not going to rest now, and neither will the British, until every last one of us is rounded up."

"You said 'now.' Has something happened?" John asked.

Genista stared at him soberly. "The Stern Gang's threatened to take out the British Foreign Secretary, Ernest Bevin."

"Dear, God! What have I gotten myself into?" John said.

"Relax, Reverend," Baharlia told him, smiling. "Who in their right mind is going to suspect, much less accuse you—a blond-haired, blue-eyed Methodist minister—of working for the Aliyah Beit?"

John shut his eyes, knowing he would need to pray about this. Then he opened them and asked, "Is there anything else I need to know?"

"Only the little matter of obtaining your entry visa for Palestine."

Late that afternoon, exhausted after his eight hour train ride, John Bark checked into the d'Angleterre on 44 Rue. The posh hotel was within walking distance to the British Embassy, but that created another problem. For during his cab ride from the station, John couldn't help but notice that the closer he got to the hotel, the more gendarmes he saw patrolling the streets…and the men he spotted lurking on every street corner, he seriously suspected were plainclothesmen.

Twenty-Three

Early the next morning, John Bark entered the British Embassy decked out in his full clerical attire which included a large cross dangling from a chain around his neck. Every guard, as well as several men John suspected were agents of the British Secret Service, had saluted him as he passed by.

Silently praising the Lord, he strolled up to the desk. "Good morning, monsieur. I'm here to apply for a tourist entry visa."

"And entry visa for where?" the clerk asked, bent over his paperwork.

"Palestine," John told him.

The magistrate raised his head and peered at John over his horn-rimmed glasses. "Palestine is a dangerous place, Reverend. I wouldn't advise it. Should you get yourself killed, our government will have a lot of explaining to do."

John smiled at the clerk affably. "The Lord will protect me. After all, it is the Holy Land, is it not?"

Not impressed, the clerk shrugged. "Have it your way, Reverend. But I'll need to cable the Palestine police for their approval before I can process your paperwork, and you will need to cover the cost of that up front."

"That's not a problem." John reached for his wallet. "How long will the entire process take?"

"Usually a week, but that's if we don't run into any problems."

ℵ

Over the next four days, on the outskirts of Paris, John Bark and Shulamet met every morning in smoky back rooms with various high-ranking members of the Hagenah. In the evenings, they rendezvoused with former members of the French underground who were assisting them to equip the *Warfield* for taking on refugees.

On the morning before John was scheduled to pick up his visa, Shulamet phoned him in a panic. "Don't say anything. Just meet at the Palace de la Concorde as soon as you can."

Thirty-five minutes later, when he knocked at her door, she yanked him inside. "We've got problems. All Jews are now suspect. You and the others must leave Paris before this evening."

"Not without my visa, I'm not."

"You don't understand! Secret police are everywhere now, and more are on the way. You must return to Marseille tonight! The *Warfield* is no longer safe here."

"I can't leave without my visa. Now, calm down, Shulamet. I need to think."

Meaning, of course, that he needed to pray, John crossed her suite and stared out of her eighth-floor window. On the street below a flashing neon billboard caught his attention. He smiled and turned around. "How many of us are in danger?"

"Eight plus you. Why?"

"The opera is performing *Thais* tonight."

"So…?"

"So, we're going to hide in plain sight."

"At the opera?"

"All nine of us in one row," John said. "When it's over, each of them can take a different route out of town."

"What about you?" Shulamet asked.

"I'll go back to the hotel, pick up my entry visa first thing tomorrow, then take a train to Marseille."

ꕥ

The next morning, in a private car on the train, John changed out of his clerical attire and back into his khakis. He was feeling pretty triumphant until he reached the dock and got out of his cab. The *Warfield* wasn't there. As John was praying about what he should do next, a French sailor approached him.

"Reverend Bark?"

"Yes."

The sailor flashed a secret hand sign to let John know he was with the Hagenah.

"Where's the *Exodus*?"

"British Intel was photographing her, so Ike Aronowitz sailed her to La Spezia, Italy."

"Ike?"

"He's your new skipper."

"What happened to Captain Johnson?"

"He went back to the States when things got too hot here, but don't worry. Ike is a seasoned sailor."

John knew that to be true. Ike had been with them since Baltimore. "What about me? What am I supposed to do?"

"Your agent is on his way to take you to the *Hatikvah*. The Portuguese ran her out of Lisbon and now the French want her gone too."

Twenty-Four

On the first of May, when the *Hatikvah* docked in La Spezia, Italy, Captain Ike was waiting for John on the pier. "I guess you heard about us being surveilled. British Intel shot us from every angle imaginable, then handed out copies to our crew. They wanted to make sure we knew what they were up to."

John stopped walking. "Are you kidding me?"

"Hold on! It gets worse. They sent a communique to the British Embassy in Washington and one to our State Department."

"What did it say?" John asked.

"That they had overwhelming evidence we're preparing to smuggle immigrants into Palestine."

"So now what do we do?"

"We keep moving," Ike said, pulling out a pack of French cigarettes. "Now that you're here we'll head back to Port-de-Bouc in the morning."

"Back to France?"

"To the south of France. And don't worry. We won't be there long, only until we decide if we want to complete our final outfitting in the Gulf of Genoa or in Monte Cristo."

ꝏ

After two days in Port-de-Bouc, the *Warfield* set sail again, this time dropping anchor in the Gulf of Poets, off the quay of a medieval fishing village in Portovenere, Italy.

John Bark looked around at the picturesque village where Lord Byron had spent so many of his vacations basking in the sun.

To John's left, tiny pastel houses dotted the hills in neatly tiered rows. On his right, a wall of rock reached for the heavens. If only his wife could have been here to see this, John mused as Steven Greenbaum came up behind him.

"The Aliyah Beit's headquarters isn't far from here."

John turned around. "That's probably why they chose the place."

"Personally, I was hoping for Monte Christo, but I kind of like it here…it's got character."

John shot him a sardonic look. "More than a lot of people I've known."

"Hey, listen. I hope you're not sore about what I said to you in Ponta Delgada. I got a little hot under the collar that day."

"Only a little?"

Steven returned John's smile. "Okay, so it was a lot."

"Ah, forget it. You're forgiven," John told him.

"It's just that with you being a Methodist and all, well, the truth is I didn't trust you, not at first."

"And you do now?"

"You've earned my respect after what you pulled off in Paris, Reverend."

John smiled. "I know I'm not Jewish, Steven, but the Messiah I serve is, and rest assured, I consider His people to be my people."

"You really believe that stuff, don't you?" Steven asked.

"I said it, didn't I?"

"Then why is it that… ahh, never mind," Steven said with a wave of his hand.

Disappointed, but wise enough to wait on God's timing, John let it go. "Well, if you change your mind, you know where my cabin is."

Steven glanced around looking uncomfortable. "Our leadership's considering embarking our passengers here."

"That's what I've heard, too," John said. Then an awkward pause elapsed between them.

"Well, I better go," Steven told him. "But I'm glad we had this chance to clear the air."

"Me, too," John said. Then he got an idea. "Hey, I'm gonna go check out the village. Wanna come with?"

"Sure! I was about to do the same."

"Did you know that Lord Byron used to vacation here? So did Tennyson."

Steven grinned smugly. "Guess that's why it's called Gulf of Poets."

John laughed as the two men synchronized their steps.

ꙮ

"Is he there?" John checked his watch. "It's almost nine."

"Keep your shirt on," Captain Ike told him, scanning the hill to their right. "He will be."

"But how do you know?"

"Let's just say we have a very well-placed…well, speak of the devil!" Ike grinned as he handed John his spyglasses. "See for yourself."

On top of the cliff to their right an officer in a green beret bearing the insignia of British Intelligence peered back at John through binoculars.

"Well, I'll be darned!" John smiled then passed the binoculars back to Ike.

"We have an operative on their staff."

"Who is he?" John asked.

"They're bivouacked in the house Shelly used to rent."

"But who is he?" John asked him again.

"Some local who works for the Hagenah."

"I know, but in what capacity?"

"I told you! He's a spy."

"But what does he do for the British?"

"He's their house boy," Ike said as Steven Greenbaum and Bernie Markus joined them. "You know how the Brits love to be waited on."

"What are you guys up to?" Steven asked.

Instead of answering, Ike passed him his field glasses.

"Holy crap!" Steven said, after refocusing the lens. Then he passed the glasses to Bernie.

The first mate looked alarmed. "They're surveilling us here, too?"

"Don't worry," Ike said. "We've got a mole on their staff."

"Hey, I've got an idea! … be right back." Steven turned to go.

Having seen that glint in Greenbaum's eyes before, John grabbed Steven's arm "Where are you going?"

"To round up our crew," he said, grinning like that cat in the funny papers.

"What for?" Ike demanded.

"So, we can stare back at him and wave, of course. You don't want that Limey thinking he's intimidating us, do you, Captain?"

ꕥ

Thus began a daily game of cat and mouse. As soon as British Intelligence crested the hill to spy on the *Warfield*, a dozen or so of its crew stared back waving at him wildly. According to the Hagenah's mole, across the ocean, in the British Foreign Secretary's office, a game of cloak and dagger was underway. Whitehall was in a tizzy. Not only was the old *Warfield* faster than every other Aliyah Beit ship, but she could stow far more refugees.

In a panic, Whitehall sent orders to all their military units, their intelligence services, and to every single one of their diplomatic consulates in Europe: "Stop the *Warfield!* We can't allow those Zionists to deluge Palestine with any more Jews!"

Exactly three days after the *Warfield*'s waving campaign began, an Italian Navy tender swept into the harbor and dropped anchor across the *Warfield*'s bow, effectively trapping them there.

In Milan, the next day the Aliyah Beit's high command convened an emergency meeting.

Arazi, one of their top operatives spoke first. "We have to be patient. Our refugees still have a way to go before reaching the Mediterranean. So, for now, we'll keep right on preparing for them, but slowly. We don't need to make the British even more suspicious than they already are. We can start by selling all our equipment that's not essential for our mission to the locals … but only a little at a time."

John raised his hand.

"Yes, Reverend," Arazi said. "What is it?"

"Since we need to know how much weight the ship can hold why don't we use the locals to test it out?"

"Because we can't afford to hire thousands of them," he said dismissively.

"We won't have to," John assured him. "We can throw a party and invite the whole village to thank them for their help."

Arazi considered it a moment. "You know, Reverend, that might not be such a bad idea after all."

As most everyone began clapping, Steven Greenbaum jumped out of his chair hooting. "It's party time!"

Twenty-Five

Over the next seven weeks, the crew, under the ever-watchful eye of British Intel, made only a third of the modifications they would need to board their refugees. One night, however, they managed to slip aboard three prominent Hagenah agents. The first—a widow, thanks to the Nazis—was Marta Sereni, an elderly Italian Jewess who, during the war, had helped smuggle 28,000 European Jews into Palestine.

Next was an American graduate of the U.S. Naval Academy named Sha'ul Shulman, who came aboard that night to act in an advisory capacity only.

The most acclaimed by far was a twenty-nine-year-old named Yossi Harel. He, unlike the previous two, would remain aboard to act as the Hagenah's honorary Admiral to Captain Ike. Before Yossi had turned fourteen, it was reported that he'd already spirited hundreds of Jewish immigrants off Palestine's shores into the Land.

More recently, however, after packing a thousand refugees aboard the *Knesset Israel* in Greece, two British destroyers forced Yossi's ship to dock in Haifa. From there they were all deported to Cyprus, but the camp didn't hold Yossi long. He escaped and was now chomping at the bit to try again.

ꝏ

In mid-June, they were summoned to a secret conference in Milan at Marta Sereni's old villa. As John looked around, admiring the woman's massive Florentine furniture, his gut warned him that something huge was about to break.

As soon as they were all seated, Marta stood up. "Our refugees are getting closer. It's time for us to move."

John's heart began to flutter as Captain Ike stood up. "Where?" the captain asked. "We're trapped by a gunboat."

Unflustered, the elderly Italian Jewess continued. "The Hagenah has produced a document with the Italian Admiralty's crest on it. It orders that Italian frigate to move out of the way."

"What good will that do?" Ike said. "The port captain will just check it with the authorities in Rome."

"Of course," Marta said, "but that will take hours. Over half of our phone lines here in Italy still haven't been restored."

Ike shook his head, unconvinced. "I don't know…it's pretty risky."

"We have no choice," Marta told him.

Sensing he had to speak, John stood up. "I know that most of you—probably all of you—think this mission is the Hagenah's plan. But it's not…not ultimately. It's the Lord's!"

When murmuring erupted all around him, John grew more insistent. "Marta is right. We have to try. So chazak! Chazak!" John said, hoping he'd not mangled the Hebrew for 'Be strong! Be strong!' too badly.

Then Steven Greenbaum began to clap. When others around the room joined him, John sat back down and silently thanked the Lord.

ꝏ

Two weeks later, in the early afternoon of June 30th, skeptical about a communique he'd just read, the La Spezia port captain picked up the telephone and smashed the button several times to get the operator. "Yes, I need the Italian Admiralty in Rome. This is urgent!"

Wondering what he should do an hour and a half later, the port captain began to pace. If he obeyed a bogus order it could ruin his reputation. On the other hand, he thought sighing, if he failed to carry out a legal one, he would immediately be fired. Having received no return call from the Italian Admiralty, he glanced at his watch, then picked up the phone again.

ꙮ

At 2:11 p.m. that same afternoon, as the *Warfield* steamed into the open sea at full throttle, John focused his binoculars on the dock. Not five minutes later, the port captain came racing down the pier, arms flailing wildly. Then the Italian frigate that had moved out of their way began to give chase.

Two hours later, John turned to the captain confused. "Why are they still pursuing us when we're so far out of their jurisdiction?"

Ike shrugged. "Why ask me? Ask your God."

"He's your God too, or I wouldn't be here."

"Don't get your back up, Reverend," Yossi warned him as Greenbaum ran onto the bridge.

"We're about to hit a squall," he said, pointing starboard.

Yossi smiled and turned to John. "Looks like our God wants to hide us for a while."

Ike slapped John's back good naturedly. "I'll have them shut off our running lights as soon as we're inside the storm."

Early the next morning on July 1st, when the *Warfield* dropped anchor back in Port-de-Bouc, the crew got busy ripping out most of their bulkheads to make room for the five-thousand shelf-style bunks they'd have to construct under the guidance of some Italian carpenters connected to the Hagenah.

In no time it seemed, the crew had transformed the ship's sunroom into a hospital. When they began rigging 5,000 life rafts, John went down to the galley to help them set up the three U.S. Navy kettles the Hagenah smuggled aboard the night before.

ꕥ

In the galley, just before dusk on July 9th, Yossi called the meeting to order.

"Before I get to the main point, let me thank all of you. You worked like slaves to accomplish what we have in such a short time. Now for the scuttlebutt…if intel can be classified as such," he said, eliciting some laughter. "Though this puts us in more peril than ever, it should also make every one of us proud."

"The suspense is killing me," Greenbaum shouted. "Get to the point!"

More laughter erupted.

Yossi waited for it to die down. "We're no longer just another Aliyah Beit ship. Our operatives in Britain have informed us that the *Warfield* is now a symbol, one that Whitehall has sworn to destroy."

"The battle is the Lord's!" John Bark shouted.

Steven Greenbaum cheered.

Then Bernie, the first mate stood up and started applauding. Soon everyone in the galley was clapping and shouting in an ever-cresting wave.

The next night, shortly after dusk, the *Warfield* pulled up anchor then skirted westward toward a tiny port city in France, situated between Marseille and the Spanish coast. According to their Hagenah operatives, due to its tiny size, Sète was off Whitehall's radar.

ꕥ

On the outskirts of Sète, in a clandestine motor pool, Fleming Lund quivered in excitement as he climbed into the bay of a large truck then offered a hand up to Yehuda.

"Big truck, yes? How many you think hold?"

Flem shrugged.

"Seventy to seventy-five," the driver said, "depending on their size. You both should sit down. I will be making many sharp turns."

"How long will it take to reach the villa?" Flem asked.

"About twenty minutes. Then, once everyone is loaded, it will be about another half hour to the dock. Hopefully, by that time your ship will have dropped anchor. If not, we'll stand by for further orders. Any questions before I shut you in?"

"We're good," Flem told him.

Yehuda stared at the document in Flem's hand. "Says Columbia. Is fake, no?"

"Oh, it's a Columbian passport all right. The Hagenah paid plenty for them. Only the names are spurious."

"Spurious? What means that?"

"They're made up," Flem told him.

"Then Yehuda right!"

Flem smiled. "I guess you are at that."

"Have 4,000 refugees. Why only 2,000 passport?"

"To keep the cost down, I suppose," Flem said. "They'll probably collect them from those who have already boarded and smuggled them out to the ones who still need them."

ꕥ

The *Warfield* entered a labyrinth cluttered with barges, fishing boats, and small craft, guided only by light that streamed down from the hill overlooking Sète's harbor.

Ike was fit to be tied. "What was leadership thinking?" he demanded, turning to Yossi.

"Calm down. We had no choice. The British are swarming every larger port."

"I can't squeeze this ship between that sea wall and the quay!"

"Yes, you can, if we enter from the east, then skirt the breakwater on our portside."

"Then you take over, Admiral! I can't!"

"Calm down, Ike. You can do this."

"The *Warfield*'s too big, I tell you!"

Yossi tossed his hands in the air. "Have it your way, Captain."

"Well, don't stalk off mad at me. This isn't my fault."

"I'm not," Yossi said. "I'm getting John Bark."

"The Reverend? What for?"

"Somebody has to pray."

ꕤ

Thirty minutes later, the *Warfield* maneuvered a sharp starboard turn into the outer harbor then made a 120-degree ark to her left before rounding a jetty to enter the basin.

"I told you, you could do this," Yossi said with a congratulatory slap to Ike's back.

"Well, we'll never reach the mooring. I'd have to make a ninety-degree pivot then back into our slot. It can't be done!"

"Yes, it can," John Bark calmly assured him.

"Not with that tangle of fishing boats constricting us, and even if I could, we'd be trapped there," Ike said as a harbor pilot with a bullhorn pulled alongside them.

"Need help getting in?"

John nudged the captain. "See? What did I tell you?"

Ike grinned. "Reverend, you're starting to scare me."

Less than an hour later, with the *Warfield* moored safely along a stone wall, there was only one project left to do before they could start boarding their human cargo. They dropped scaffolding over the side, then four crewmembers covered the *Warfield*'s name with fast-drying paint. Before sunrise, they would inscribe the old ship with her new moniker, then hide their handiwork under tarps until they were safely out to sea. Then John would uncork the champagne he'd been entrusted with for the *Exodus'* christening.

ꕤ

It was daylight, and only half of their refugees had boarded. The Tour de France bicycle race, scheduled to end in Sète that afternoon, had solved one problem for the Hagenah but created another. Yossi, knowing that every hour of daylight boarding increased their risk, began to sweat, and it wasn't only from the humidity.

"Are you okay?" the Reverend asked him as Captain Ike walked up to them with two refugees.

"Admiral, meet Fleming Lund. He's here to chronicle our voyage."

Yossi extended his arm. "I'm delighted to have you aboard, Fleming. With the pummeling we've been taking in the press, it's high time the Hagenah had its own correspondent."

"It's good to meet you, too," he said shaking Yossi's hand. "But, actually, I'm the Lord's correspondent."

Not sure what that meant, Yossi shrugged. "Same difference, isn't it?"

"Not quite," the Reverend said, eyeing the young journalist closely. "Are you Jewish?"

"Isn't everyone aboard ship?" Lund replied, smiling affably.

"Not everyone. I'm Methodist, but my Messiah is Jewish. John Bark's the name," he said, extending his hand. "It's a pleasure to meet you."

"Likewise," Lund replied, returning the handshake. Then he turned to the kid next to him. "This is Yehuda Grünbaum. He escaped from a concentration camp in Romania."

"Well, that took some doing," Ike said, looking impressed.

"Yeshua, He make miracle. Make Yehuda invisible. Legal immigrant now."

"If you're legal, what are you doing here?" Yossi asked.

"The agent who recruited me recruited Yehuda also," Lund explained.

"To do what?" Yossi demanded.

"He never told us. Why? Is that a problem?"

"I don't know," Yossi said. "But you can't stay with the refugees."

"I can throw down a couple of mats on the deck in my cabin," the Reverend offered.

"That'll make for some pretty tight quarters," Yossi said, wishing

John had kept his nose out of it.

"No tighter than steerage," Ike said.

The Reverend clapped Yehuda's shoulder. "Come with me. I'll show both of you to my cabin, then we can go scavenge some bedding."

Twenty-Six

"Anyone seen Yossi?" Ike asked no one in particular.

"He went to talk to some guy but said he'd be right back." Bernie checked his watch. "That was fifteen minutes ago."

Ike picked up the voice tube. "Okay, steam up the engines. We'll be underway in another forty minutes."

"Should I move the barges now or wait?" Bernie asked.

"Now! I don't want anything holding us up once our engines are steamed."

"We've got trouble!" Yossi yelled, sprinting up the gangway, breathing heavily.

Flem grabbed his pen and opened his notebook.

"The British strong-armed the French to hold us here."

"They can't do that!" Ike bellowed as two harbor policemen bounded up the plank.

"You cannot leave this port!" the shorter one hollered. "Your certificate of sea worthiness does not cover this many passengers."

"It most certainly does!" Captain Ike shouted back.

Flem began to pray.

The policeman waved a paper. "Our order comes directly from Prime Minister Bidault."

Yossi glared back at him.

"It might be his signature, but I can guarantee you the order originated in Whitehall. You know it. And so do we."

ଌଓ

While apprehensive refugees sweltered on the upper decks, Flem entered the blazing hot galley along with the ship's crew to take notes at their emergency meeting.

"In the morning," Yossi said, "they plan on moving us up the canal, behind the drawbridge, to make sure we stay put."

"What can we do?" someone shouted.

"Four of our Hagenah agents are meeting with the maritime prefect as we speak. Another, from the Mossad, is on his way to Paris to persuade officials there."

"A whole lot of good that'll do," another crewmember said sarcastically.

"Pipe down!" Yossi told him. "Captain Ike and I have come up with our own solution. We'll be offering the harbor pilot who guided us in ten thousand dollars in francs if he'll lead us out."

"When?" someone asked.

"Tonight, if he accepts."

Flem laid down his pen and began praying silently.

ଌଓ

Flem's alarm clock went off at 4:00 a.m. Missing his bed at home, he forced himself off the thin mattress. "Rise and shine, Yehuda. We've got a busy day ahead of us."

When the youth failed to respond, Flem switched on the lamp. Alone in the cabin, he hurriedly dressed then grabbed his notebook.

He found John and Yehuda with their heads together on the deck, leaning against the rail and was about to join them when the captain started yelling on the bridge. Curious, all three went over to investigate.

"What's wrong?" John asked.

"Our engines are ready to pop their safety valves and so am I! That meshuga pilot should've been here ten minutes ago."

"Let's give him a few more minutes," Yossi said. "He still might make it."

"Captain Ash and Johnson were right. The *Warfield* is jinxed!"

Flem dug out his pen and opened his notebook.

"She's not the *Warfield* anymore, Captain," John reminded him. "She's the *Exodus* now, and God is in control."

"If that's so, why does everything always go wrong?" Ike demanded.

John clapped Ike's shoulder. "Calm down. We've made it this far, haven't we?"

Ike glared back at him without answering, then stalked off the bridge.

"We wouldn't need miracles if everything always went smoothly," Flem offered meekly. Only John and Yehuda smiled.

"Not worry! Yeshua make miracle again."

Yossi turned on him, scowling. "Listen, you. We've got over 4,000 Jews aboard this ship, and most of their family members have been exterminated by Christians. So, I wouldn't be throwing that name around if I were you."

"I use the Lord's Hebrew name all the time," John said, looking shocked. "You've even asked me to pray for you a few times, so what's your problem?"

"You're not a Jew!" Yossi retorted.

"What difference does that make?" John shot back.

Hoping it might calm the waters, Flem said, "At least Yossi realizes Yehuda is still a Jew. My father didn't accept that I was still a Jew. Not at first."

Yossi turned to him, glaring. "You're one of them, too?"

The Reverend John Bark smiled. "I suspected as much."

Flem was about to ask John about his remark when the captain ran back onto the bridge with Bernie.

"Get down to the galley, John! I need you to help Cook prepare a feast. We're wining and dining all the port guards tonight."

"Why?" Yossi demanded.

"I'll steam up the engines while we're getting them drunk."

Bernie grinned. "Then I'll strip down to my skivvies, swim out to the mole, and free our stern line."

Ike nodded. "Once the engines are good and steamed, we'll send our guests ashore with bottles of their own, to ensure they'll keep drinking, and ship out."

ՋՕ

As soon as the last port guard staggered ashore, Captain Ike gave the order. "Okay! Move her ahead!"

Flem heard the propeller kick over twice…then it died.

Ike's face turned red. "Get down there, Bernie! See what the problem is!"

Ten minutes later, he returned to the bridge, soaking wet and frowning. "The end of the cable I cut got wrapped around a screw. I tried to free it, Captain, but couldn't."

Ike reached for the voice tube. "Okay, listen up! I want you to rock the engines back and forth—slowly—just enough to dislodge our stern line from a screw."

A minute later the chief engineer called the bridge. "Propeller's cleared, Captain."

Everyone on the bridge cheered.

Ike breathed a sigh of relief.

Flem thanked the Lord, then petitioned for angels to lead them out safely. Thirty minutes later, when the ship entered international waters, John Bark removed the tarps, revealing the ship's new name. But as John was about to uncork the champagne and christen her, the officer on watch ran onto the bridge.

"We've got trouble, Captain! A British warship is on our starboard side!"

Flem lifted his field glasses just as the H.M.S. *Mermaid* flanked them, then a British Lancaster zoomed in overhead and hovered.

Twenty-Seven

When the sun rose the next morning, the British were still stalking them. Yossi switched on the public address system.

"Boker tov! We're headed for Palestine. But before you start celebrating, I must inform you of the challenges we're facing. They'll require self-discipline on your part and organizational skill on ours. With so many of you aboard, constant shifting of weight can make the ship unstable. I'm restricting movement in large groups from one side of the ship to the other. I've appointed a detail to control our traffic flow. A galley detail will transport meals to your assigned areas then collect your dirty dishes." Yossi paused. "I must also let you know, since most of you have already spotted them, that His Majesty's ship the *Mermaid* has been giving us a royal escort ever since we entered international waters. But don't let them intimidate you. One way or another, we'll get you into Palestine. Well, that's all for now," Yossi said, then switched off the P.A. system.

ജ്ജ

On their third day at sea, Flem wasn't sure if what he felt was seasickness—the Mediterranean was choppy—or if he'd eaten too much of last night's pemmican, a survival staple made from dried beef, suet, raisins, and brown sugar. But he quickly found out the hard way. So did two hundred or so others. With mounting cases of diarrhea, the sanitation detail was kept busy. Refugees and crewmembers alike had to stand in line for hours to use the trough-style toilets.

The stench was horrific, Flem wrote in his journal, but after a few days it finally passed and no one died. Now everyone on board, except infants and nursing mothers, are busy performing their assigned duties. In the afternoons, Hebrew classes, as well as many vocational ones, are provided to help refugees adjust to their new lives in Palestine.

The ship's milieu is a mixed bag, Flem wrote, of Orthodox, Conservative, and Reform Jews, even many agnostics and atheists. Young and old, the formerly prosperous and the poor, artisans, laborers, scientists, physicians, professors, some crackpots, and even a few thugs have one thing in common: They all long to have their exile ended.

John Bark rushed into the cabin and shut the door. "We need to pray!"

"What's going on?" Flem asked, closing his composition book.

"Now three more ships have joined our royal escort."

ꕥ

On the bulkhead overlooking the stateroom, Flem watched as two crewmembers from the Bronx printed bold letters in Gothic: "Men who once fought for freedom now fight those fighting for freedom!"

Moved by the salient irony, Flem opened his notebook and recorded it for posterity.

ꕥ

Early that afternoon, a hundred and twenty-five miles south of Crete, the sea got suddenly choppy. The old ship began to sway.

When Steven Greenbaum charged into the galley like a bull, Flem looked up from his journaling. John, sitting across from him, set his spud and peeler down on the table.

"What's wrong, Steven?" Flem asked.

"We need to slow down. Our superstructure's shifting again. Its scaring the crap out of the refugees."

"Have you told the captain?" John asked.

"He knows. He can feel how rough it is."

"I mean about our passengers and slowing down."

"And have him take my head off? No thank you!"

John exchanged smiles with Flem, then stood up. "I'll go have a talk with him."

"Mind if I tag along?" Flem asked, shutting his notebook.

"Sure. The more the merrier."

They reached the bridge as Yossi signed off from his daily radio update with the Mossad in Tel Aviv.

John cleared his throat. "Our superstructure is shifting again, Skipper."

"What's new about that?" Ike asked, not bothering to look up from his charting.

"The passengers are getting anxious. Don't you think we should slow down?

"You after my job, Reverend?"

"I'm only making a suggestion, Captain," John said humbly.

Captain Ike opened his mouth to reply but his first mate caused it to shut again when he ran onto the bridge red-faced.

"We've got four more now, Skipper—the *Ajax*, the *Chieftain*, the *Chequers*, and the *Charity*."

"Are you kidding me?" Ike yelled.

But before Bernie had the chance to assure him he wasn't, the commanding officer aboard the H.M.S. *Ajax* picked up his bullhorn. "You are carrying illegal immigrants. If you try to enter Palestinian waters, we shall board you! Do not resist! We are a far superior force."

ꕥ

The next morning when another British frigate, the H.M.S. *Cardigan Bay*, joined the royal flotilla, Steven Greenbaum birthed another one of his bright ideas. As soon as Yossi declared it to be brilliant, Flem positioned himself on a small deck that gave him a bird's eye view of the drama about to unfold below.

This time when all the British officers lined up on their main deck with field glasses to inspect them, the crew of the *Exodus* fell into formation on the deck to show them they weren't intimidated. On cue, when the famous march known as "Pomp and Circumstance" began blasting at top volume over their public address system, the mostly American, straight-faced crew mockingly flashed the British officers the Royal Navy's palms-down salute.

The crew was cheerful after that, until the afternoon when another emergency meeting was called, this time on the bridge with only a few select participants. Flem prayed silently as their contingent waited anxiously for Yossi to sign off with the Mossad in Tel Aviv.

When he finally did, Yossi exhaled heavily before turning to address them. "We only have one viable option. Push her to twenty knots as soon as we're right outside of Palestine's territorial waters. With the *Exodus'* shallow draft we can beach her close to the breakers. The British won't risk their destroyers going in that far. So, tomorrow evening, just before 6 p.m., six miles off Tel Aviv, we'll beach her south of a red brick building. To save us time, all who can swim will have to reach shore on their own. The rest will go in lifeboats. Our rescue team will meet them there. We should be able to unload in under an hour. Any questions?"

When no hands shot up, Yossi continued. "If the unthinkable happens and the British board us illegally at sea, we won't resist, at least not with firearms! As soon as we're done here, I'm sending a team of you to search our passengers and make sure there aren't any weapons. Should you find any, dump them overboard. There are several Aliyah Beit agents aboard, including me, and we're all wanted by British Intelligence, so we'll go into hiding. We created a space behind the refrigerator box in the storeroom. It's stocked with water, rations, toilet paper, and buckets."

"How will you get off the ship?" Flem asked.

"A cleaning crew is coming aboard as soon as the British give the all clear. When they start singing in Hebrew, we'll come out of hiding."

Flem raised his hand. "What about Haifa's security?"

"Along with supplies, the cleaners will be bringing extra janitor uniforms for us to change into."

"And our refugees? What about them?" John Bark asked. "Are we going to just abandon them to the British?"

"We're not abandoning anyone, Reverend! A new agent, one British Intel doesn't know about yet, was embedded with them back in France. Just pray it doesn't come to that!"

ꕥ

When the weather turned foul the next day, forcing the *Exodus* to slow down, the Mossad pushed beaching time ahead another hour and changed their landing place to a few miles down from Tel Aviv just south of Bat-Yam.

Mesmerized by the sea's churning, Flem leaned over the rail wondering what might happen if they failed to pull this off.

"You okay?" John Bark asked. When Flem turned around, John frowned. "Don't bother to answer that. I can see it in your eyes."

"What if things don't go the way we want them to?"

John placed his hand on Flem's shoulder. "What was it Paul said? 'To live is Christ, to die is gain.'"

"You can say that—you're a widower. I have a wife, a child, and one on the way."

"Relax, Flem! The British can't be any worse than the Nazis. You stood up to them, didn't you? God is still in control, so don't go wobbly on us now!"

"I know He's in control, but what if His plan isn't the one we think it is?"

"It'll still be His plan, Flem, whether we interpret it right or not, and you'll still be His journalist."

"You're right," Flem said as the cloud over him lifted. "Eliezer told me I would write my articles after this mission."

"Who's Eliezer?" John asked.

Flem hesitated. "I can't tell you right now, but if you aren't doing anything important why don't we go back to the cabin? You haven't told me the full story of how a Methodist pastor got tapped to be chaplain aboard the Hagenah's *Exodus 1947*."

ꙮ

At the Mossad suggestion, Captain Ike set a course for the coast of Egypt to test the Royal Navy's willingness to pursue them into shallower waters. A little before 6 p.m., with their royal escort flanking the *Exodus* on both sides, they hit the three-fathom line a little outside of Alexandria's territorial waters. As soon as Captain Ike gave the order to inch the keel toward the bottom slowly, the British flotilla dropped astern of them seaward. Then they spread out and shut off their running lights.

Captain Ike grabbed the voice tube. "Alright, now reposition our trajectory toward Beit-Yam's breakwaters! Full speed ahead!"

The second the *Exodus* entered Egyptian territorial waters, the lights aboard the British destroyers came back on. As Ike barked out orders like the skipper of an eighteenth-century man-of-war, the *Exodus'* crew got busy spreading wire mesh over the promenade deck and every exterior opening in case the Limeys boarded them. They stacked sandbags in the wheelhouse to prepare for flying bullets and ran a pipe from the engine room onto the main deck through which they could pump oil.

Near midnight, Flem went down to the galley to grab some coffee to help him stay awake. When he returned to the bridge, a thick fog had rolled in.

"Why don't you catch a little shuteye?" Ike suggested. "I'll wake you if it looks like something's about to break."

Glad for the suggestion, Flem quickly complied.

ﬁ

At 4:30 a.m., Captain Ike shook Flem's shoulder. "Rise and shine, Lund. We're twenty-three miles off the coast of Palestine!"

Thirty minutes later, as the ship's bell struck five, searchlights lit up the *Exodus,* and its whistle began to shriek.

The battle was on now, and a dozen teenagers charged onto the hurricane deck screaming. Captain Ike turned to John. "You and Flem get up there and shut those brats up before they have everyone hysterical!"

"You have entered Palestine's territorial waters. Turn off your running lights and prepare to be towed!"

Ike flipped on the PA system and turned the volume up all the way. "You're a liar! We're still in international waters. If you board this ship, it will be an act of piracy, a violation of maritime law and you'll have to answer to the United Nations. We have 4,500 Jews aboard—men, women, and children—who'll not abide by any law that forbids them—forbids us—to enter our God-given land, and we're not going willingly to another concentration camp, not even one run by you bloody British!"

Ike flipped off the PA system. "Tell them to bring her about," he told the first mate. "We're reversing course."

A minute later, two refugees hoisted the Magen Da'vid on the upper deck, fore and aft.

Flem's heart burst with pride.

Then gunfire erupted.

"Relax! Those are only firecrackers," Ike told him as teenagers draped a canvas Flem had seen the youths working on earlier in the week over the rail on the hurricane deck. The caption read: "England, this is your enemy!" Depicted beneath the lettering was a mother holding her bundled infant.

Twenty-Eight

When the H.M.S. *Childers* rammed them portside, the *Exodus* lurched starboard. Trapped between the destroyers, their only chance of escape was to gun the engines toward Bat Yam. But as Ike grabbed the voice tube to communicate that to the wheelhouse, the H.M.S. *Ajax* swooped across their bow.

Flem watched dazed as the Royal Navy, on both sides of the ship, lowered drawbridges. In less than a minute, British sailors and marines were swarming the decks armed with carbines, machine guns, and battering rams. The refugees resisted with whatever they could lay their hands on. Bottles, oars, even cans of meat became flying missiles.

Unmolested by the Brits, Flem hurried to the main saloon to check on the youths. When he got there some older teens were ripping the spindles out of the grand staircase and handing them to the younger ones to use as clubs for protection. He scribbled a few notes then went up to the hurricane deck where eight of their crewmembers were engaged in fisticuffs with five of the British invaders.

After forty minutes of making rounds and taking notes, as if unseen, Flem returned to the bridge just in time to witness three Royal Marines wrest Bill Bernstein from the wheelhouse.

Undaunted, Bill grabbed the fire extinguisher and charged back in. Only, this time, a blow from a royal blackjack stopped him. Bernstein hit the deck.

As the assailants were vacating the wheelhouse, John Bark ran up behind him, and Flem's fugue-like-state lifted.

"I'll get his hands. You get his feet."

"Where are we taking him?" Flem asked.

"Ike's cabin's on the other side of the chartroom."

Finding it empty, Flem relaxed, then noticed the captain's chart to Bat Yam open on his desk. "Do you see what I see?"

"Ike's cabin is right through that door. Let's take care of Bill first."

When they returned a few minutes later, a pair of British officers were conversing quietly in a corner of the chartroom.

"You distract them," John whispered. "I'll take care of the chart."

Flem nodded, then cleared his throat. "Excuse me, I'm with the *Copenhagen Gazette*. We have a sailor in the other room who was bludgeoned and needs a doctor."

"Who are you? What are you doing on this ship?"

"I just told you, I'm a journalist. Would you like to see my credentials?" Flem held out his press card and passport.

While the officers examined them, Flem glanced over his shoulder. As John crumpled the incriminating evidence, Flem started coughing to cover the sound. Then John shoved it into his pocket.

"They seem to be in order," the taller officer said, handing them back to him. "But Intelligence will have to clear you before you can leave the ship."

"What about Bill Bernstein? He needs a doctor!"

"He'll be transported to our hospital in Haifa," the officer said dismissively.

"Don't you have a doctor aboard one of your ships?" John asked.

The ranking officer turned around then stared at John's cross. "Who in hades are you? You're certainly no refugee."

John extended his hand. "I'm Reverend John Bark." Neither of them shook it. "Would you like to see my entry visa?"

"Not now. Intelligence will investigate both of you thoroughly in Haifa."

ꕥ

As soon as the battered *Exodus* moored alongside a crowded pier in the port city of Haifa with the *Childers* at her bow and the *Providence* at her stern, the crew and refugees lined up on the promenade deck and began singing the Jewish anthem, Hatikvah.

Then the Reverend John Bark reached his palms toward a group of glaring Army officers on the pier and blessed them ceremonially. When he finished, he turned to Flem. "Do you see those two in white suits over there? The gentleman to the right is Justice Emil Sandstrom. He's the chairman of the United Nations Special Committee of Inquiry on Palestine. That guy next to him is Vladimir Simic, a Yugoslavian delegate. You and I need to have a chat with them."

"Are you kidding? The British aren't going to let us within spitting distance of either one of them."

John smiled. "I'd bet you, if I were a betting man, that the Hagenah already has."

"Reverend Bark, come down here immediately!" a British officer with a bullhorn demanded. "And bring that Danish reporter!"

Five minutes later, another officer shoved Flem and John into the back of a military vehicle then whisked them off to a heavily guarded police station. After several hours of being interrogated, they surrendered their visas and, compliments of the British Mandate government, were checked into the Savoy Hotel.

The officer in charge handed John the room key. "We will notify you when the date of your deportation hearing has been set. Until then, you need to stay put. Both of you!"

Eager to let Liesel know some of what happened, Flem dialed the operator. After a sweet but short conversation, he clicked for the operator so he could call Geørg.

Then someone knocked at the door. Flem hung up the receiver. "It's Steven Greenbaum and Yehuda."

John rushed over and let them in. "How'd you know where to find us? And why weren't you two jailed with the others?"

"We slipped away while they were occupied," Steven replied cockily.

"Not slip away, Steven! Yeshua do miracle!"

Greenbaum rolled his eyes. "You and your miracles."

Flem flashed John a smile. "Well, come in and make yourselves at home. There's fresh fruit on the credenza," he said pointing. "Help yourselves if you're hungry."

John shut the drapes. "Any word about Bernstein's condition?"

"We lost him an hour ago," Steven said soberly.

Flem sighed, feeling nauseous. "I was afraid he wouldn't make it. I can still hear the awful sound made by the blackjack against his skull."

After that, no one spoke for several seconds.

Then Steven went over to the credenza. Inspecting the bowl of fruit, he said, "A hundred and forty-six are injured, and twenty-eight of those are in critical condition."

"What about our refugees?" John asked as Steven selected a peach.

"They're on their way to Cyprus as we speak."

"Who's been giving you all these statistics?" Flem asked, brokenhearted by the enormity of all their failures.

"Eliezer!" Yehuda said.

The hair on Flem's arms stood on end. "He's here in Haifa?"

"Who is that guy anyway?" Steven said. "He's kind of weird, isn't he?"

"He's the reason Yehuda and Flem are both here," John informed him.

"What else did Eliezer tell you?" Flem asked.

"Where to find you, for one." Steven said. "He also confirmed what Yossi told us about the Jewish Agency sending in a cleaning crew."

"Did Yossi and the others get away?" Flem asked, encouraged by the news.

"They did," Steven confirmed grinning widely, then frowned. "Is Eliezer in the Hagenah?"

Flem shook his head to the negative. "Just very well-connected, to use his own words, but I have to confess, I'm really surprised the British agreed to a Jewish cleaning crew."

"I'm not," Steven said. "Those dandies wanted no part of having to clean up the mess they made. They wanted to rub our noses in it as a lesson not to thwart them again. But mark my word, by tomorrow, Yossi, Captain Ike, and all the others who went into hiding will be back in the saddle!"

"Well, we won't be," Flem said. "John and I have deportation hearings to look forward to."

"Maybe have," Yehuda said, then turned to Steven. "Tell what Eliezer say."

"A couple of big-time newspaper men, both Americans, will be escorting you to a house in Jerusalem tomorrow."

"What for?" Flem asked.

"You and John are to meet with Guatemala's ambassador to the U.N."

"Jorge Garcia-Granados?" John asked, shooting Flem an excited glance.

"Our Leadership wants you answering all of his questions. Tell them exactly what happened … and when."

John clapped Flem's back. "What did I tell you? The Hagenah never misses a beat!"

"Who are these American newspaper men that will be escorting us?" Flem asked.

Steven shrugged. "Sorry, I can't remember their names, but one of them works for the *Palestine Post*."

ꕥ

The next morning, when the knock they'd been expecting rattled their door, Flem reached into his pocket for a coin. "Want to flip for who answers that?"

"The honor's all yours, Flem. I just wanna see the guy's face if he's who you think he is."

When Flem opened the door, Mordi Ginzburg stood there alone.

With an emotionless expression, he said, "Good to see you again, Lund. I hear you and Reverend Bark have been having yourselves quite an adventure."

"That's one way to put it," Flem said. Trying not to look too vindicated, he opened the door wider. "Please come in. We were expecting two of you."

"Yeah, well, something came up at the last minute," Mordi explained as he extended his hand to John. "You've become quite a legend, Reverend."

John laughed. "Not to mention the bane of Whitehall's existence. I can't understand why the British never expected to find a minister of the gospel aboard a Hagenah ship. What about you, Mr. Ginzburg? Were you surprised to learn that Fleming Lund got tapped to chronicle our voyage?"

Ginzburg glanced at his watch. "It's getting late. We better go. We don't want to keep Granados waiting."

ഈ

The interview lasted exactly one hour and forty-three minutes. "I want both of you back here tomorrow," Granados told them as he showed them the door. "Emil Sandstrom, the Chairman of the UN Security Council on Palestine, will be here as well as some others. You will need to assure them of two things, and two things only. Where was the *Exodus* when the British boarded and was anyone armed?"

The next morning, an hour before they were to leave for their appointment with UNSCOP, a knock sounded at the door. When Flem opened it, he was only slightly surprised to find Eliezer standing there smiling at him. "Come in before someone sees you."

The old man entered calmly.

As Flem shut the door, John rushed into the room.

Eliezer extended his arm. "Pleased to finally meet you, Reverend."

"This is Eliezer," Flem explained.

"To what do we owe this pleasure?" John asked the old gentleman as they finished shaking hands.

Eliezer removed a large manila envelope he'd tucked under his arm and handed it to John.

"What's this?" John asked.

"Evidence, all the evidence you'll need to prove our case."

An hour and twenty minutes later, Flem and John assured the other council members that they'd searched the entire ship for weapons and found none."

"The problem is your location," Emil Sandstrom said, unsmiling. "It boils down to your word against the British."

"No, it doesn't," John said then handed him two documents.

"What are these?" Emil asked.

"The *Exodus'* taffrail log and logbook. The cleaning crew found them in the ship's ballast. Bernstein, the young man the British clubbed to death, always stowed them there for safe keeping.

"They confirm everything we've told you," Flem assured him. "It's tangible proof that the British boarded us illegally in international waters."

ꙮ

As soon as the indisputable facts were printed as a headline in the *Palestine Post*, the Yishuv rejoiced. In Cypress, according to reports, refugees cheered for nearly twenty minutes. From there, news that the British Navy had illegally boarded the *Exodus* spread around the globe like wildfire, sending Whitehall's Ernest Bevin into a rage.

The next day, bending to popular demand, the British freed every *Exodus* crewmember who was being held behind bars in Haifa. They also dropped all charges against John and Flem and returned their entry visas.

ജ്ര

"Excuse me, Lieutenant General, the overseas operator has your party on the line."

The high commissioner of Palestine picked up his phone. "Bevin, this is Sir Alan Cunningham. I've called to warn you that should you take any reprisals against the *Exodus'* refugees, so help me God, I will make your life a living hell!"

"Don't you see what they're pulling?" Bevin yelled back.

"You broke international law, you idiot! You've ruined our reputation, made us a laughingstock."

"Those stiff-necked Jews need to be taught a lesson, and so do the bloody French! I don't care what you say, I'm sending them all back. Let France clean up the mess. They made it!" Bevin slammed down his receiver.

ജ്ര

"You look discouraged," Devorah told Flem as he walked into the kitchen, "like you've lost your last friend."

"I feel like it," he said. "We have four-thousand refugees crammed aboard three British transports headed back to France. How much more can those poor souls take?"

She opened the cupboard. "Maybe a nice cold drink of water will help," she said as the phone began to ring. "Would you mind answering it, Flem? If it's Magda, tell her I'll call her back."

Nodding, Flem picked up the receiver.

"I have a person-to-person call for Fleming Lund. Is he there?"

"You're speaking to him," Flem said, hoping it was Geørg returning his call to approve the vacation he'd requested.

"Flem, my boy, pack your bags!"

Flem relaxed. "Thanks, Geørg! I haven't seen my family in weeks."

"Then you can take three weeks off as soon as you get back."

"Get back? Back from where?"

"I want you in Port-de-Bouc, France when your refugees dock. Your flight out is at 10 a.m. tomorrow, so make sure to hit the sack early. Our circulation's increased thirty percent in just a few weeks, so keep up the good work."

ꙮꙮ

Nodding off for nearly an hour on the plane had made Flem's lack of sleep the night before more bearable, but he was still groggy when his cab dropped him off at the dock an hour after the British transports had moored. He flashed his press card to the port guard.

"I'm Fleming Lund, with the *Copenhagen Gazette*. I'd like to interview the Jewish refugees."

"Well, that won't happen. They've refused to disembark."

"Then may I go aboard one of the ships?"

"Sorry. We have orders. No visitors allowed until they call off their hunger strike and start to cooperate."

Flem was about to ask if he could interview the port authority, then changed his mind. "Would you be so kind as to call me a cab? Mine just left."

"Be glad to," the port guard said and picked up his phone.

Tomorrow, Flem would pay a friendly visit to Georges Agustin Bidault, the president of the French Provisional Government. Considering all the negative press the man had been getting for the fiasco he'd helped to create, Bidault just might be willing to pull a few strings to get Flem an interview with some of the refugees if he promised to write something flattering about Bidault in one of his articles.

Twenty-Nine

"I am sorry, monsieur," Bidault's young secretary informed him. "The president is in a meeting with our Minister of Information. But if you would like to take a seat, I'll be sure to let him know that you're here when they're through."

Flem shrugged. "Why not? I've nothing better to do."

"If only I could say such a thing. I'm so behind on my mimeographing. So, if you will excuse me, I'll get back to it now."

"No problem," Flem told her as she rushed out of the office. He picked up a magazine but as he was about to sit down, the muffled voices coming from behind the president's door grew loud and angry.

"I don't care what those Jews want, Pierre! His Majesty's Government wants them off those ships!"

"That might have been possible had the British not lied to them about going to Cyprus."

"I don't care about all of that. Just get them to disembark!"

"I'm sorry, Georges. I've done all that I can…legally that is. I've offered them asylum in five different languages—Yiddish, Hebrew, German, English, and French. They refuse to budge."

"Then drag them off in chains!"

"Monsieur President, if spewing such nonsense makes you feel better, by all means continue. But do not think for one moment that your ranting can alter international law."

"What are you talking about?"

"Nationals from other countries—even Jewish ones—cannot be forced to embark on foreign soil."

ꕤ

Sickened by what he'd just heard, Flem left Bidault's outer office before either man had time to come out. As he walked the streets, he pondered what to do. Then it dawned on him. He didn't need to reveal how he became privy to the information, only that he did and that his sources needed to remain anonymous.

Over the next few days, Flem's article became a two-part story. And by the following week it turned into a series of columns, written, of course, from the point of view of the 4,451 displaced Jewish holocaust survivors sweltering aboard three British transports, who refused to disembark anywhere except Palestine.

British Foreign Secretary Ernest Bevin, the vindictive brains behind sending the *Exodus'* refugees back to France, was choleric, fit to be tied, according to the piece Flem read in the *London Lite*.

Then on August 21st, the British Colonial Office in Palestine sent a registered ultimatum to the Jewish Agency. If in twenty-four hours the refugees still refused to disembark, all three of the transports would set a course for the British-controlled zone in Germany, where the British would then forcibly remove every Jew to a German Displaced Persons Camp.

That next morning, the dock in Port-de-Bouc teemed with reporters and cameramen filming their newsreels. Next to Flem, a journalist from the Chicago Tribune pointed to the H.M.S. *Empire Rival.* "Look! They're forcing a white flag out of that porthole."

As more of the bedsheet billowed in the breeze, Flem smiled. "Better look again." Printed in French on the sheet were the words, "To Palestine! Liberty! Equality! Fraternity!"

When most of the reporters on the dock began cheering, the refugees aboard began shouting joyfully as a lone female voice yelled, "We love you, France! But tell the British to send us home to Palestine!"

Then, at the masthead on the H.M.S. *Empire Rival*, three refugees ran the blue and white Magen Da'vid up the flagpole and all the refugees aboard began singing Hatikvah.

ꕥ

A little after 3:00 p.m., five French government automobiles and two ambulances pulled onto the pier, causing some in the press to scatter.

"What's going on?" Flem asked, rushing over to one of the ambulances. "Is someone sick?"

Ignoring him, the driver and the orderly accompanying him removed two gurneys from the back of the vehicle as a throng of reporters surrounded it peppering both attendants with questions. Answering none of them, the men shoved their gurneys up the gangway of the H.M.S. *Ocean Vigour.*

A minute later, a reporter standing nearby yelled, "Look! They're abandoning ship."

Flem turned to his right. Sure enough, refugees, mostly older ones, were wobbling down the gangway of not only the *Ocean Vigor* but the other two transports as well.

Flem could hardly believe what he was witnessing until a representative of the French Provisional Government announced through his megaphone that sixty Jews were ill. Those able to walk would be driven to the hospital in government cars. The rest were being transported by ambulance.

The vigil continued until 6:20 p.m. Then, bound for Germany, all three of the British transports pulled away from the harbor. Disappointed by the outcome, Flem took a cab back to his hotel to pack, reminding himself that in less than a month his wife would give birth to their second child. As for everything else, he prayed that God's will would be done.

ꕥ

Two days later, as Flem was drinking coffee, waiting for Liesel to pick him up at a bistro outside the airport in Cyprus, he heard a radio newscaster announce that a man named D.N. Pritt had served six writs of habeas corpus, two on each of the three British transports when they stopped to refuel in Gibraltar. Under orders from Whitehall, each of the three captains refused to submit. One of the skippers was reported to have said that neither hateful reporting nor legal action nor anything else would prevent them from delivering every last one of the Jews to the British Zone in Germany.

ꕥ

"To prevent sabotage, we must keep our train routes secret. Those vultures out there would love nothing better than to pick the meat off our bones, so let me do all of the talking," Colonel Percy Hastings warned his subordinate as he opened the door to a gaggle of journalists armed with microphones and flashing cameras.

Hastings threw his hands in the air. "Please! Hold your questions until I've delivered my remarks then you won't need to make so many inquiries." When they quieted some, he continued. "As ordered by our Central Commission, we will be providing ration cards to the refugees for necessities before Army Intelligence screens each of them over the next two weeks."

"Two weeks?" someone shouted. "Why so long?"

"We must determine which of these Jews are actual victims of the Nazis and which of them are members of the Hagenah. Those who refuse to cooperate with us will have their ration cards voided."

"Why treat them like criminals? All they want is what Balfour promised them over twenty years ago."

"If they refuse, are you going to force them off at gunpoint?"

"If necessary, we're prepared to employ three degrees of compulsion: Tear gas, water hoses, and manhandling," the colonel said, choosing to answer the less pernicious of the two questions.

"Only as a last resort shall we call in our troops."

Enraged, the media began shouting slurs. Then a reporter four feet away from the colonel gave him a Nazi salute.

Infuriated by the rabble's uncalled-for hysteria, Colonel Hastings made a hasty retreat with his subordinate in tow.

ꟹ

On September 4th, when three more British transports joined the flotilla in the Straits of Dover, a dense fog rolled in, forcing them to slow down, so their estimated time of arrival got pushed forward to Monday, September the 8th.

The H.M.S. *Ocean Vigor* reached Germany first. The officer in charge grabbed his bullhorn. "For your own safety, I implore you to disembark from the ship peacefully!"

After a heated debate about whether to leave the ship or not, they finally agreed. Then 2,500 British soldiers armed with clubs and tear-gas herded them through a long chicken wire passageway into train cars with wire mesh covering every window.

ꟹ

The H.M.S. *Empire Rival* arrived in Germany early the next morning, and this time all 1,406 of its refugees left the ship immediately. But at 10:00 a.m., when the H.M.S. *Runnymede Park* docked, all 1,485 of its refugees refused to budge until three hundred military police, wielding clubs and firehoses, stormed the vessel.

After two hours of resisting with whatever they could lay hold of, most of them finally surrendered. The few who didn't were dragged ashore forcibly. But in spite of their physical defeat that evening, they triumphed. Every time British Intelligence asked who they were and where they were from each and every refugee named a famous biblical character and listed their country of origin as Israel.

Not wanting to incur any more wrath from the international press, the British reneged on their threat to revoke ration cards for noncooperation.

ꕤ

Nearing midnight on September 21st, Flem banged on his father-in-law's door. "Liesel's water just broke. What should we do?"

"Stay with her! I'll be right there."

Heart pounding, he dashed back in to find Liesel up pacing the floor and holding onto her abdomen. Thinking it not wise, he took hold of his wife's elbow and was leading her to the bed as Deidre rushed in.

"Good girl! Walking helps you to dilate. Would you get me some clean sheets?" she asked, turning to Flem.

Relieved that someone with experience had taken charge, Flem brushed past Dr. Prestur who was on his way in as Flem ran out into the hall.

"What's going on?" Caleb asked, peeping out of his bedroom.

"The Lord's about to bless you with a little brother or sister. Now go back to bed. We're all busy right now."

"Can't I help?"

"You can, by staying out of the way." Seeing the hurt in Caleb's eyes, he quickly added, "and by praying for your mother and new sibling."

Four and a half hours later the most perfect eight-pound, three-ounce female entered the world, and as predetermined by her parents, should their second child be a daughter, they named her Naviah, which in Hebrew means prophetess, a seer of heaven.

ꕤ

By November 29, 1947, all of the *Exodus'* displaced Jews who had been deported to Germany emigrated to other countries. A few returned to France, others found asylum in the United States but the majority, determined to reach Palestine, reconnected with the Aliyah Beit. Their plight had become a symbol that filled hearts around the globe with a fervor for justice. Tonight, Flem hoped that zeal would inspire all the delegates of UNSCOP to vote in favor of partitioning Palestine.

"It's me. Can I come in?" Aldur asked, not bothering to wait for an answer.

"What do you think of my new home office?" Flem asked.

Aldur looked around approvingly then sat down.

"I took Liesel to see *Casablanca* last night."

"Great film. Did she cry?"

Flem nodded. "She did at the end when Rick told Ilse they'd always have Paris before sending her back to her husband. But those aren't the lines that will forever be etched in my memory."

"What are they? 'Round up the usual suspects?'"

"It's when Rick tells Ilse that he's not good at being noble, but the problems of three little people don't amount to much in this crazy world—meaning, of course, that beating the Germans did."

"That was good, but my favorite is still when that Nazi, I don't remember his name, said they were closing Rick's Café because of the illegal gambling, then someone hands him his winnings."

Flem smiled. "Rick made the right decision. Let's hope that the UNESCOP delegates make the right one tonight." Flem stood up. "Ready to go down?"

Aldur flipped open the lid of a jewelry box. "I picked this up earlier this afternoon. Do you think Julie will like it?"

"It's beautiful," Flem said. "Have you shown Liesel and your parents yet?"

"I didn't get the chance. Julie wanted to take a walk with them before dinner, and Liesel was much too busy. You know how she loves to play hostess. I was hoping you could distract her when they get back so I can show them."

"Just leave Julie to me," Flem said as they headed down the stairs.

"Are you nervous about tonight's vote?"

Flem frowned. "Maybe just a little. After all, it wasn't that long ago I was positive we were going to smuggle 4,500 refugees into Palestine."

"World sentiment has changed since then," Aldur assured him as they entered the parlor, "and the United Nations knows it."

"Yeah, well, it's too bad the British still don't," Flem said frowning. "Can I pour you a libation to celebrate your engagement?"

"Whatever you're having will be fine, but Julie still has to say yes."

"She will," Flem assured him as he grabbed a bottle of Moscato. "Sometimes I think the British are deranged. They've lost all sense of decency."

"Their credibility is certainly in the hopper after claiming there was no room for them in Cyprus, then not two weeks later finding space for several thousand more."

"Ernest Bevin wanted his pound of flesh and everyone knows it."

"The Americans certainly do," Aldur said smiling.

Flem handed him a glass of wine.

"Your piece about Senator Morris' letter to their Secretary of State was sublime."

"Which one?" Flem asked. "I wrote two."

"The one comparing Palestine's Jews to the colonists in the American Revolution," Aldur said. "But what I don't understand is why every Jew isn't a Zionist. You would think they'd all want their land back."

Flem frowned as he poured a drink for himself. "A prominent member of the American Council for Judaism, a very anti-Zionist group, recently told Jews in America that dual allegiance was dangerous. He called Jews like me and Christians like John Bark extremists," Flem said as the front door opened.

"Don't forget to distract Julie," Aldur whispered.

"I won't," Flem promised as they walked into the room. "I'm so glad you could join us tonight, Julie," he said, greeting her with a kiss to the cheek. Then he linked his arm through hers. "Come with me. There is something in my mother's garden I've been dying to show you."

ꕥ

"Dinner is now served," Liesel said, curtsying in the doorway.

Heart pounding, Aldur stood up. "Before we eat, Liesel, there's something I have to do and I want all of you to be my witnesses." Aldur dropped to one knee and held out the ring. "Will you marry me, Julie Abercrombie?"

She gasped and covered her mouth, staring at the emerald cut diamond.

"Say yes, Miss Julie!" Caleb prompted after several seconds of silence. "Say yes!

"Yes! Yes, of course, I'll marry you!"

Aldur relaxed.

"Well, go on, Son," his father urged him. "We're all family here, so there is no need to be shy. Kiss my future daughter-in-law."

"Kiss her! Kiss her!" Caleb began chanting as Aldur slipped the engagement ring on Julie's finger.

Then he took her in his arms. Twenty seconds later, his mother cleared her throat. "You can stop now, Son. We all want a chance to welcome Julie into the family."

Reluctantly, Aldur let her go.

ꙮ

Liesel grabbed both of her brother's hands. "Now repeat after me. My sister was right about Julie, and I'll listen to her advice from now on."

Aldur grinned and turned red. "Touché, Sis!"

"No…you have to say it!"

"My sister was right about Julie..."

"Keep going," Liesel prompted.

Then Naviah began to wail and Aldur smiled. "Your daughter wants you."

"Well, don't think you're getting out of this. I'll be back!" she warned then turned to the others. "Why don't you all go into the dining room while I go up and check on Naviah. We have to be finished with desert no later than 9:45 or we'll miss the opening of tonight's vote."

"Roger's going to call after the vote," Julie said, "to let us know what the Yishuv's response is."

"Well, have him reverse the charges. I'll put it on my expense account." Flem smiled. "That is, if you let me interview him first."

"By all means. Only, don't mention my ring," Julie said, gazing at her hand, then she smiled up at Aldur. "I want to tell him myself."

ꕥ

After dinner, as the others were taking their seats in the parlor, Flem tuned the radio to the BBC, then finetuned to eliminate the static.

"The ad hoc committee of tonight's United Nations' rollcall vote will now begin," the chairman announced. "All those in favor say 'yes.' Those against 'no.' Abstainers, well, you know what to say." When the laughter died down, he commenced with the rollcall.

"Afghanistan? No! Argentina abstains. Australia? Yes. Belgium? Yes. Bolivia? Yes. Brazil? Yes. Byelorussian S.S.R.? Yes. Canada? Yes. Chili? Chili abstains. China abstains. Columbia abstains. Costa Rica votes yes. Cuba? No. Czechoslovakia? Yes.

When the chairman announced that Denmark voted yes everyone in the parlor applauded.

"Dominican Republic? Yes. Ecuador? Yes. Egypt? No. El Salvador abstains. Ethiopia abstains. France? Yes. Greece? No. Guatemala? Yes. Haiti? Yes. Honduras abstains. Iceland? Yes. India votes no. Iran? No. Iraq? No. Lebanon? No. Libera votes yes. Luxemburg? Yes. Mexico abstains. Netherlands? Yes. New Zealand? Yes. Nicaragua? Yes. Norway? Yes. Pakistan? No. Panama? Yes. Paraguay votes yes. Peru? Yes. Philippines? Yes. Poland votes yes. Sweden? Yes. Saudi Ariba votes no. Syria? No. Turkey? No. Ukrainian S.S.R. votes yes. Union of South Africa? Yes. United States of America? Yes. U.S.S.R.? Yes. United Kingdom abstains."

"No surprise there," Julie said as everyone around her booed.

"Uruguay? Yes. Venezuela? Yes. Yemen votes no. And

Yugoslavia abstains."

They all sat on the edge of their seats, exchanging tense looks as they awaited the final tally.

Then the chairman cleared his throat. "It looks like we have thirty-three in favor of partitioning, thirteen against, and ten abstentions."

Flem rushed back to the radio as the chairman declared, "Palestine will be partitioned!" and switched it off before some blathering BBC commentator could start lamenting the result.

"Let's pray!" Flem said as everyone bowed their heads.

"We praise You, Adonai, for what You've done, are doing, and will do. Your Word informs us that the natural always comes before the spiritual. Min smukke," he said, turning to Liesel, "would you hand me my Bible please?"

Finding the prophecy he wanted to read, he began again. "At present, Adonai, we Jews who worship You are only a remnant of a remnant. But Scripture declares that one day Israel's dry bones will come to life and be filled with Your Holy Ruach."

Then Flem began to read. "'I prophesied as You commanded and there was a noise … behold a great shaking! Bones drew near, bone to bone. I beheld sinews and flesh come upon them, and skin from above began to spread on them.'" Overcome by emotion, Flem paused. "'But there was no Spirit in them.' " He looked up from the page. "This, Yeshua, is the condition of most of Your people today. But a day is coming when an even greater miracle than what happened tonight will occur. Once the fullness of the Gentiles has come in, Your people, my people, will cry out, 'Baruch habah b'shem, Adonai! Blessed is He who comes in the name of the Lord!' On that day, Yeshua, Ezekiel's prophecy will have come to fruition and all Israel will be saved." Blinking away his tears, Flem finished the rest of the prophecy from memory.

"'Prophesy, son of man! Say to the Spirit, 'Come from the four winds, O Spirit! Breathe on these slain ones so they may live.' On that day, as it says in the book of Romans, life will come from the dead. I thank You, Yeshua, for bringing us here to witness to Jews like Steven Greenbaum and Mordi Ginzburg, who love the Land You gave us but do not know You, the Keeper of Israel, Who sent them here. But You warned me not to despise small beginnings, so I won't. I, that is we, will just thank You for tonight's miracle vote."

As everyone was saying amen, the telephone began to ring. Julie jumped up from the sofa. "Would you mind if I answer that, Flem? Then I'll give it to you."

"Be my guest. Just don't forget to have the operator reverse the charges," he said.

Thirty

"It's been crazy around here ever since the vote got tallied," Roger said as he gazed out of his third-floor window. "I can hardly hear myself speaking."

"Are those car horns I keep hearing?" Flem asked him.

"And fireworks. They light up the sky about every two minutes."

"I really wanted to be there, but I had a promise here to keep."

"I understand completely," Roger told him.

"How's your Mandate government handling the result of tonight's vote?"

Roger sighed. "Most think Israel will be wiped off the map as soon as we pull out, but I think they're also relieved to finally be leaving the mess they've created here."

"What about you?" Flem asked him. "Do you think they'll drive us into the sea?"

"Politics is a byproduct of faith, Flem. Don't forget that we have Christian Zionists in our ranks as well and that three years ago, hundreds of our soldiers and sailors went on a hunger strike to protest the disparity in our immigration quotas, and that divide still exists even amongst members of our cabinet."

"Thanks. I needed to be reminded of that, Roger. Well, I better get off now, your sister's shooting me dirty looks. She has something she wants to tell you, so I'll say goodbye for now and shalom."

"Same to you," Roger said as his sister came on the line.

"Guess what I'm wearing on my left hand?"

There was a brief silence, then Roger whistled. "We'll it's about time! Have you set the date yet?"

"My enlistment is up in January, so it will be soon after that, I'm sure."

"Then you've decided for certain not to reenlist?"

"Our troops are pulling out. I'm not! Aldur and I will be staying in Palestine."

Roger was about to correct her when he heard Aldur say, "We'll be staying in Israel. It won't be Palestine much longer, Julie."

ℰ𝒪𝒞𝒮

"While we're all still celebrating," Flem said. "I have some more great news to share with you. My folks have decided to immigrate to Israel. Father has wanted to for quite some time, but with quotas being what they were, Mother wouldn't discuss it. Now, along with world sentiment, all that's changed. My mother is now fully on board and so is my cousin Inger."

"That's wonderful, Flem!" Deidre said, excitedly. "It'll be like old times. We can have big family gatherings again."

"I want to read you something," Flem said, opening his father's latest letter. "'"As you know, Son, Katlev was the bane of my existence. I blamed him for everything, especially for losing you, or thinking I had. Then Rabbi Jacob Mitzger opened my eyes, and Yeshua did the rest. So as soon as we get our land back all three of us will be making Alyiah."'

Flem's eyes blurred, making it difficult to focus, but having read it so many times he quoted the rest from memory. "'"Soon we Lunds will be worshiping our Messiah in the land…For the rest of our lives the Lund family will worship our Messiah in the land of our patriarchs. I'll get to hold my granddaughter, Naviah, in my arms and hear Caleb call me Zayde again. And although it breaks my heart that dear Jacob won't be with us, I'll finally get to know Katlev's third musketeer, Rabbi Matityahu Goldberg and his delightful wife Devorah.'"

Epilogue

The next day, on November 30, 1947, after rejecting the United Nation's partition plan to create both an Arab and Jewish state, Arabs blew up the Jewish commercial center near Jaffa Gate. Thus began Israel's War for Independence.

The gerrymandered partition the U.N. laid out looked like a checkerboard. Sixty percent of their allotted territory would be in the Negev desert, and Israel's borders would be indefensible. But those weren't the fledgling nation's only problems. The Jews would now face an internal threat as well, thanks to decades of the British Mandate government's unrestricted Arab immigration.

Living amongst the start-up population of 597,000 Jews, would be 397,000 anti-Semitic Arabs determined to drive every last one of them into the sea. And Israel's orthodox Jewish community living in the Holy City would be effectively cut off because the U.N. had decided to make Jerusalem an international zone under their control.

After two thousand years of exile, Israel finally became an independent nation-state on May 14, 1948. Then, early the next morning, five standing armies—from Lebanon, Syria, Iraq, Jordan, and Egypt—advanced on the Holy City. But He Who keeps Israel—Yahweh Elohim—never sleeps nor slumbers (Psalms 121:4).

The End

Author Bio

In her own words.

In 1952, I was born in Key West, Florida, which I'm sad to report no longer exists except in my memories. Unlike today's Key West, my hometown was family oriented. It was a small Navy town located at the southernmost tip of the Florida Keys, known best for fishing and for one very prolific and famous author, Ernest Hemingway, who lived, fished, and penned many of his novels there between 1929 to 1939. I often wonder now if this bit of history might've been what first inspired me to write. But it wasn't until after I came into covenant with the God of Abraham, Issac, and Jacob, that my love of writing became a passion. When I wasn't devouring *how-to-books* on writing fiction I was putting into practice the skills I'd learned. My first two attempts were awful. My third showed improvement. But it was my fourth, *Miracle Across the Sound*, a historical novel about ordinary Danes who smuggled most of their Jewish countrymen to safety across the Sound into neutral Sweeden in 1943, that I knew would be published. And it finally was in 2021, nearly seventeen years later, after I'd turned what started out as Christian fiction into a new genre that I've dubbed Hebrew Roots Christian fiction. And now, nearing the end of 2023, I am happy to report that my sequel to *Miracle Across the Sound*, titled, *A promise Broken A Promise Kept*, has been published by Little Roni Publishers.

More Messianic Titles from LRP

5-Star Fiction

Pick up your copy today,
ebook, softcover & hardback.
Exclusively at Amazon.com from
CONTENDING FOR THE FAITH
Betrothed
Messianic Imprint of
Little Roni Publishers
Grow closer to the Lord, learning more about Him
daily. Contending for the Faith is a wonderful tool
in helping us understand our Heavenly Father & King.

Pastor E. Herschberg
Pastor Clay Adkins
Revelation 9,11
A Timely Commentary on CERN, Hell, & Darkness
Amazon
#1 New Release
Messianic Judaism
#CERN
#HELL
#ALIENS
Have scientists opened portals to hell?
Rabbi Eric Herschberg & Pastor Clay Adkins Discuss

Betrothed
Messianic Imprint of Little Roni Publishers
ALABAMA | TENNESSEE
www.littleronipublishers.com

Little Roni Publishers' *Betrothed* Imprint has been created and set apart to the glory of Yeshua Ha Moschiach, our God and King.

Isaiah 58:12 | Galatians 2:20

Made in the USA
Middletown, DE
15 October 2024